SAVIORS

OF THE BUGLE

Barbara Elmore

Mud Pie Press

Published by: Mud Pie Press
4201 Morrow Ave.
Waco, Texas 76710

© 2003 by Barbara Elmore
Book design by Chandra Moira Beal
Cover design and illustration by Vern Herschberger

Printed in the USA

Library of Congress Control Number: 2001119163

ISBN: 0-9714941-0-X

Summary: Led by a classmate, middle school students try to save their town's newspaper.

To journalists everywhere.

To readers who keep newspapers in business.

To supporters of the First Amendment.

To sister Kathy Smith, thoughtful teacher, editor, supporter.

To friend Carolyn Davis, talented writer, fierce editor, eternal friend.

To Don, whose creativity and independence are an inspiration.

Barbara Elmore, a veteran journalist, is also the award-winning author of *Breathing Room* and *Crookwood*. She lives in Waco, Texas, with her husband, Don, an artist.

CONTENTS

One

Score 2 for Mom

Wendy laughed out loud at the "Cheeky and Claude" comic strip. Then she remembered and glanced over her shoulder. Had Wanda heard? She held her breath momentarily, listening, before letting her eyes wander back to the newspaper.

Claude was a Great Pyrenees and a detective. Today he was having trouble tying his trenchcoat. Cheeky — a young boy named for his round cheeks — told Claude he needed to lose some weight. "No time for that nonsense," growled Claude. "Besides, who would trust a skinny Great Pyrenees?"

"He's right," Wendy muttered, reading the strip a second time. A skinny Great Pyrenees was like a skinny cook. The flowing, fluffy white hair made the breed look round even if they weren't. She thought the cartoonist had done a good job of getting down the boxy shape of the dog's head, too, especially for a comic strip. And the round, dark eyes looked so real that Wendy peered into them.

Wendy would like a dog. But Wanda would never stand for that.

She thumbed through the newspaper until she got to Mrs. Ramsey's column, "All I Know," which was always on Page five. She forced herself to read it. "Hmmpph," she grunted after a moment. "Should be called 'I don't know anything but I've got to fill up this space.'"

"Are you reading that silly *Bugle*?"

Wendy jumped, pinching the tops of her thighs on the table underhang. Her mother breezed into the kitchen. Any kind of warning – an approaching footstep or a creaking floorboard – would be nice. Or a bell, like some people put on their cats. Wanda always appeared out of thin air and moved without a sound. And seemed to know everything.

"Did we know Maxwell Silver?" Wendy asked.

Her mother frowned. The *Bugle* came on Wednesdays and Saturdays and Wendy asked her about something in it every chance she got, hoping to find a subject that would snag her interest. Wanda hadn't wanted anything to do with the *Bugle* since Miranda was gone.

"Maxwell who?"

"Silver. He lived on Birdwell Avenue."

"No. Are you reading the obituaries again? That's morbid. Please put the paper away."

There would be no *Bugle* delivered to the Wright house anymore if Wendy's father Terry didn't insist. He would read it front to back and wished out loud that it was a daily paper. Wanda would reply that Moffatt Corner obviously didn't have enough news for twice a week, judging by what it reported now. And Terry would ask what she expected for a town of seven thousand. "More," Wanda always said.

"Bacon and eggs, Wendy? Two or three, and scrambled or

over-easy?"

"Just cereal, Mom. I can get it myself."

"I can see you've been reading about diets again. I won't let you go to school unless you eat something substantial. How about scrambled eggs, bacon and toast? And a muffin. I made blueberry yesterday."

Wendy tried to focus on the obituaries, but her eyes traveled downward to her wide thighs. They were stuffed into her jeans like sausages, and looked broader spread out on the chair than they did when she was standing. She had just bought the jeans two weeks ago, and they already felt too small.

Why couldn't Wanda understand what it was like to be fourteen and fat? Why couldn't she help her lose weight, instead of forcing bacon and muffins on her? She had been different when Miranda was around. All her attention wasn't focused on Wendy then.

The full plate landed right on top of the obituaries.

"Aren't you going to eat?" asked Wendy, eyeing the bacon hungrily as she attacked the pile of eggs. They were done just right. If only her mother were either a bad cook or a fat one, everything would be all right. But Wanda Wright was a size eight. She was tall and had the kind of figure people described as willowy. Wendy was sure she wouldn't have liked her in school. Never trust a skinny cook, she thought, and smiled.

"I'll eat later, after I take you to school." Her mother pulled the newspaper from under Wendy's plate and folded it in half, then folded it again into a narrow, rectangular sliver, before placing it out of Wendy's reach. "You shouldn't get so attached to this newspaper, Wendy. It may not be around much longer, so I hear."

Wendy's fork stopped in mid-air. "What?"

"Don't talk with your mouth full," said her mother, frowning. "It's just a rumor, so don't get all excited."

Wendy counted to ten, then twenty. She would count to thirty before demanding to know the story. As she got to twenty-eight, her mother spoke.

"I overheard two men talking about it at the grocery store yesterday. One was saying that some big advertiser is pulling out his ads, and apparently that will take a huge chunk of the *Bugle*'s budget. I really didn't pay that much attention. Eat your breakfast before it gets cold. You don't want to be late."

"But why? Why would you pull an ad? Who was the advertiser?" Wendy eyed the rectangle of newspaper and wished she could reach it. She wanted to look at the ads.

Her mother shrugged. Wendy pushed her plate away. She didn't feel full, but sort of sick, as if she were coming down with something. She wanted to be by herself. She wanted to call the *Bugle* office and demand to know if what her mother said was true.

The *Bugle* had been a part of Wendy's life since before she could read. She'd stayed inside much of the time with Miranda, who couldn't play outside like other children did. One thing they could do together was look at the *Bugle* and laugh or cry at the stories.

At first, Wendy only looked at the pictures. When she'd gotten old enough to understand the comics, Miranda read them to her. When she was eight, she started reading the whole paper, or at least her favorite parts, by herself, although she and Miranda still read parts of it together. When Miranda's column started appearing, she felt like she owned part of the *Bugle*.

"Are you through eating already? I wish you would eat everything. There's nothing I can do with a muffin and few bites of egg," said Wanda as she whisked the scraps went into the

4

garbage disposal. "Get your books and I'll drive you to school."

"Could I please walk? It's not that far and I need to think."

"That's not safe."

"It's Moffatt Corner, Mom!"

"Get your books and let's go."

And that was that.

The elastic waist of the jeans dug into Wendy's belly and the denim pinched her upper thighs as she stood. She got her books, then peeked into Miranda's room as usual. Everything was in place, and the shade was up. Just the way she'd liked it. Thin morning sunshine streamed into the window, and Miranda's chair was pulled out slightly from the writing table, which held her notepad and three sharpened pencils.

Wendy pulled the door shut.

She and her mother rode silently down Tumbleweed Lane to Third, then a mile to Riddle Middle School. Seeing the rhyming name on the front of the school almost always cheered Wendy, but not this morning. Even the excitement of finding herself a pound lighter this morning had faded away. That was before Wanda's bacon and eggs. She'd probably put on three or four pounds in the last hour.

The *Bugle* rumor, also courtesy of her mom, sat as heavily on her insides as the eggs and bacon. She hoped with all her heart, which must be big since the rest of her was, that it wasn't true.

As she kissed Wanda on the cheek, a scoreboard popped up in her head: Wanda 2. Wendy 0.

Two

Pot, Pooh, and Spot

Libby and Riley were waiting for her at the school entrance. She gave her mother a peck on the cheek and scrambled to make a fast getaway. Her mother was faster. "Be sure to eat a good lunch," instructed Wanda as Wendy got out of the car. The school menu said mashed potatoes today. You need the carbohydrates. And comb your hair. It's a mess!"

Wendy nodded and tried to smile. Her stomach felt better as she watched her mother drive away.

Wendy didn't even say hello to her friends before telling them what her mother said about the *Bugle*.

"But why would it close?" asked Libby. "And how could it close? Doesn't Moffatt Corner have to have a newspaper?"

"It's not required by law," Wendy said. "Mom said something about an advertiser who was mad at the paper."

"But I still don't understand," said Libby, shaking her head. "How can one person matter enough to make a newspaper close?"

"Good question," said Wendy shrugging. She looked at Libby's dress. It was pale pink and made of material that had little nubs on it, with puffed sleeves and a sash tied in a bow in the back. An eight-year-old would love it. Libby's mother must have gone shopping again.

"Don't even say it. Mom and I had a big fight over this dress. Guess who won?"

"I kind of like it." Riley had held back until then, listening to them talk about the *Bugle*.

"For who? Your four-year-old sister?" Libby snapped.

Riley ignored the remark. They all knew he didn't a have a four-year-old sister. "The color is nice on you."

"It really isn't so bad," Wendy said, going behind her friend to undo the bow. "Now wrap this around the front and tie it there." She nodded as Libby retied the sash in the front. "That's better. And Riley's right. The color is great. If only…"

"If only I could get rid of the sleeves, the full skirt and the sash, it would be fine, right?"

"Well," began Riley.

"Yes," finished Wendy.

Libby was beautiful despite her clothes. At age two, she won the annual Moffatt Corner Baby Beauty Contest. Her mother, a pretty woman herself who had moved to the United States from France, had been buying Libby's clothes and trying to enter her in beauty pageants ever since. Only when Libby started taking ballet did her mother let up. Libby hated ballet, too, but not as much as she hated beauty pageants.

Most of all, she wanted to be like everyone else, which was hard because she wore children's clothes but was mature beyond her fourteen years. She spoke French fluently, thanks to her mother's insistence, and she could type a million words a minute because her mother operated a home-based typing service, which Libby helped with during busy times. Wendy and Riley were the only other people who knew of Libby's talents

8

besides her mother. Libby thought if anyone else knew, they'd think she was weirder than she looked.

Riley cleared his throat, and Wendy saw he had books stuffed under each arm. He was struggling to hold them but would never ask for help.

"Good grief," she said, grabbing two which she handed to Libby, then three more, which she tucked under her own arm. "Why do you have to bring all your books at once?"

"Because they're all due today. Thanks," he added, turning red.

"Dare I look at the titles?"

He shrugged his thin shoulders almost up to his ears, which looked bigger than normal because he had just gotten his short hair cut again. His parents insisted on a cut well above Riley's ears and buzzed all around, and Riley didn't seem to care. The sun glinted off the spiky top and made his hair look even redder than usual.

Wendy didn't have to look at the books to know they all had something to do with science, engineering or history. Riley was most happy amidst his books, half a dozen Fig Newtons, and a bottle of ginger ale.

"I've heard Dad talking about somebody who's fighting with the paper, but I don't know who," said Riley. "But I do think one advertiser can make a big difference to a newspaper, especially in a small town like this. If you lost a lot of money and couldn't pay people, or couldn't buy supplies, you might have to close. Nothing personal. I like the *Bugle*," he added hastily.

"Let's just drop it, ok?" Wendy said as they headed to class. She needed to get her mind off the subject, but that was not to be. The *Bugle* came up again in her first-period government class.

Her favorite teacher, Mrs. Martino, was talking about censorship as it concerned a new book and used a story she'd cut

9

out of last week's *Bugle*. Wendy was immediately engrossed. She'd read the story in the *Bugle* herself.

"I want us to talk today about censorship as it pertains to schools," said Mrs. Martino, "the books you read, and the books someone decides you should not read. I hope this exercise will get you to think. The book I want to talk about today is titled *Ehab*."

Someone snickered, and Mrs. Martino paused before continuing. "How many of you know about it?"

Everyone was silent as Mrs. Martino walked from desk to desk, looking hopefully at the top of students' heads. Wendy couldn't let the teacher down. She raised her hand.

"Yes, Wendy?"

"I haven't read the book, but I read that newspaper story. I had a lot of questions about it, but not very many answers."

"We can get to your questions in a moment. But first, could you sum up what the newspaper story said for those who didn't read it?"

Chewing on her lip, she thought for a minute. "The book is about a boy who moved to this country from the Middle East and has trouble being accepted by his classmates."

"Yes, that's right," said Mrs. Martino. "Did you understand why some parents didn't want their children reading the book in class?"

"Some people didn't think their children ought to be reading about a Muslim, but I wasn't sure why. I don't understand what a Muslim is."

Before Mrs. Martino could answer, someone began muttering in the back of the room. The teacher looked toward the sound, and it faded away.

"Without going into much detail, I will tell you that a Muslim is a person of certain religious beliefs."

"Yes," said Wendy, "and that's why some of the parents didn't want their children reading about Ehab. His questions about Christians upset them, according to the story."

"That's right," said Mrs. Martino, nodding. "I don't think it's important for us right now to discuss what Muslim beliefs are. I want us to talk about censorship — the definition of the word, what it means in a public school —"

She stopped and looked toward the back of the room. Burnam Horton Jr. had raised his hand.

"Yes, Burnam?"

"I thought we were studying government. What does that newspaper story have to do with government? We don't even know if the story is true. My dad says you can't believe anything that's in the *Bugle*. Or any newspaper!"

A hush filled the room as everyone looked at Mrs. Martino. She nodded.

"I understand, Burnam. But we have to have a starting point for a discussion, so we are going to assume for the purposes of this class that the story is true." She paused and looked around the classroom.

"Now, who can answer Burnam's question about how this issue relates to government?"

Wendy studied the pencil on her desk. She had said enough for one day. Let someone else talk. Someone who wasn't a fat know-everything.

"Wendy, how about you?" asked Mrs. Martino.

She stared at the pencil a moment longer, then looked up. She felt eyes staring at her and knew everyone was waiting to see how she would connect the newspaper story with government class. She took a deep breath. "The class that was reading Ehab was in a public school, and public schools are supported by taxes that people pay." She kept her eyes on the pencil.

"And people are the government. At least in this country."

Nobody said a word for a moment, and she wondered if they could all hear her heart beating. "Yes, that's right," said Mrs. Martino, her face beaming. "Very good, Wendy." Then she looked to the back of the room. "Burnam, does that answer your question?"

Wendy glanced at him. Burnam Horton said mean things almost every day, and had pet names for lots of the kids, including her. He hung around with five or six other boys who laughed at his jokes and followed all of his instructions, including playing tricks on people. Their most recent prank was to lock Herman Koos, who was small and quiet and wore his brother's too-big, hand-me-down clothes, in the janitorial supply closet. Herman was in there a whole day before anyone found him, and was too scared to tell anyone how he got locked in. But everyone knew.

Burnam's pet name for Wendy was Pot. Libby was Pooh, and Riley was Spot. She guessed she ought to be glad his pet names for them weren't worse. Then there were the rumors that Wendy tried to ignore because they seemed like an excuse for his behavior. Burnam, who was tall and skinny, always wore long-sleeved shirts, winter and summer. People said it was to hide the bruises and scars or his arms. Wendy didn't know about that. She just knew that Burnam was a royal pain.

As she glanced at him, she noticed how wide his smile was and braced for the worst.

"It took so long to get an answer, I forgot my question," he said. Laughter erupted and seemed to last forever. Wendy blushed a deep red. In her embarrassment, she barely heard anything else during the rest of the class. She hurried out of the room when the bell rang. Libby and Riley finally caught up to her at her locker.

"What's your hurry?" Riley asked.

She threw her government book into her locker and grabbed another book. "I wanted to get out of there. I felt stupid for answering that question about government after everybody laughed."

"They weren't laughing at you," lied Libby. You gave a great answer."

Riley nodded.

"I don't think we were in the same room," Wendy said. "See you guys at lunch."

She hurried off. They had classes elsewhere, so she knew they wouldn't follow. They were only trying to make her feel better, but she wished they wouldn't. It made her feel worse when her friends felt sorry for her. She sat at the back of the room in all her classes the rest of the morning and didn't volunteer any information.

By lunchtime, she'd managed to block first period and the *Bugle* out of her head. She found a table in the cafeteria, and Riley and Libby joined her a few minutes later. She was afraid they'd bring up first period again, but neither of them did. They ate pizza while talking about "Alarms Going Off," a new song by Intense Women in Tents, and "Painted Driveway" by the Four-Nerve Daisies. Then Libby and Wendy talked about Marcy Street's outfit. Riley ate a dill pickle and looked around the room. He ate a pickle every day, even with spaghetti or egg rolls.

"I read a fashion story that said those tight-legged pants are out," said Wendy, eyeing Marcy's hot pink knit pants. "The new look is flowing clothes."

"I think I'll start reading the paper, too," said Riley. "Maybe not fashion stories, but other stuff."

"Why do you read it , Wendy?" asked Libby.

"I just like it," Wendy said with a shrug. Libby and Riley

were her best friends, but she didn't want to talk about Miranda and her columns.

Their conversation was interrupted by a voice nearby.

" You like that rag? I bet your diary is a cure for insomnia!"

Wendy felt her face get hot. She sat perfectly still.

"What's the matter? No smart answers now?"

She looked at Burnam Horton. "This is a private conversation! Anyway, why would I waste any words on you? You wouldn't know a smart answer if it slapped you!"

Burnam's lower lip trembled as if he were going to cry and he faked the sniffles. "Ouch, Pot! That hurts!" He gave a fake sob. The boys with him snickered and Wendy turned away.

"You don't have to look at me but you should listen," he said then in his normal voice. "You'd better read the *Bugle* while you can! My father says it won't be around much longer."

"You don't know everything!" Wendy responded.

"Maybe not, but my dad knows about this. His ads are in there twice a week."

"That doesn't mean he gets to decide if it closes!"

"Who do you think pays for the *Bugle*, Pot? You think just because you pay a quarter for it twice a week, you're supporting it? Well, you're not! The advertisers decide everything! And since my dad advertises more than anyone else, you figure it out!" Horton smirked as he got up. "Pot, you and Pooh and Spot have a wonderful day," he added.

"Sorry, guys," muttered Wendy to her friends as they all stared at each other.

Riley ran a hand over his face, paler than usual, which made his freckles stand out even more. "Don't worry about it."

Libby rose with as much grace as her puffy sleeves and flouncy skirt allowed. They left the cafeteria silently, keeping whatever they were thinking to themselves.

——— Three ———

Older Than Dirt

Burnam Horton Sr. owned Horton's Hardware. The oldest of three children, he was sole owner of the business that had been established by his grandfather and passed down to his father, an only child.

As townspeople told the story, the elder Horton, a stern man who had also been the mayor of Moffatt Corner for two decades, had intended for all three of his children to share equally in the business, but that never happened. Burnam Sr. gradually took it over, establishing himself as buyer, seller and keeper of the books. In the end, even his own father was shut out of the business he had run for forty years. There were rumors that he was forbidden from even visiting the store, and he died soon after he sued his eldest son for fraud and the lawsuit was dismissed. By that time, he was no longer powerful in Moffatt Corner. Everyone was afraid of his son.

Horton Hardware had operated in the same well-kept stone building since the late 1800s. It was the oldest continually operating business in Moffatt Corner, and "Horton" was a household word. Shoppers had been known to ask for a Horton wrench, and sentences often began with, "I need to go to Horton's and get…"

It also was the only hardware store in Moffatt Corner. Burnam Horton Sr. had seen to that by staying on the Chamber of Commerce's New Business Committee. Anytime a similar business might be looking at moving in, he would buy the property before anyone else had a chance. The one competitor who had managed to sneak into town stayed in business fourteen months before Burnam Horton cajoled or threatened his customers into returning to Horton Hardware.

You had to drive thirty miles to Marlett to find another hardware store, and you didn't want Burnam Horton Sr. to find out if you did. He'd been known to ask customers to leave the premises if he'd heard they had shopped in Marlett.

Burnam Sr. was six and a half feet tall; his neck was as thick as a telephone pole, and his hands were as large as hams. He greeted people who entered his store in a voice that sounded like thunder, always with the same friendly-sounding words: "How can we help you today?" He refused to let customers shop without "help," which usually meant getting cozy with the smoldering cigar that dangled from the corner of his mouth. The way he treated customers, and the rumors about how he treated his wife and only son, meant that a lot of people would rather drive the thirty miles and risk Horton's wrath than shop at Horton Hardware.

It wasn't hard to believe he would threaten to close the *Bugle* for some real or imagined insult, but he wasn't mentioned when a *Bugle* story one Saturday morning told its readers that it was on shaky ground. The paper would close, said the story, unless it could cut expenses enough to make up for a loss of revenue.

As she read the story, Wendy held her breath. The headline said:

'Bugle' fights
money woes
Loss of revenue forces newspaper
to make tough decisions

The story was really a letter from the editor, Luella Cathcart.

"We are forced to make tough decisions this week at the *Bugle*. We are laying off employees in an emergency attempt to remain in operation. In coming weeks, our readers will see changes in syndicated features, in how we cover events, and in the size of their newspaper. We will no longer carry some features, and the paper will shrink accordingly.

"We hope our faithful readers will stick with us as we try to correct our financial problems and strengthen our position. We will continue to cover the news, and we believe we will emerge from this trial a stronger newspaper."

As Wendy hurriedly turned the pages to see if "Cheeky and Claude" was still there, she wondered who the editor meant when she wrote "we." If she had laid off employees, could there be a "we" left?

Wendy paged to the back of the first section, where the comic strip always was. The strip was not at the top of the page. In its place were two stories that were really advertisements. One was about a new piece of road equipment available for cities, and another was about a lawn tractor. Both had big pictures beside them, and both were available at Harvey's Machinery in Marlett.

Finally, at the bottom of the page, she saw "Cheeky and Claude." "Oh thank you, God," she breathed. But her relief

17

was fleeting. This wasn't the usual funny "Cheeky and Claude." The big dog was ill, lying flat on his side as he told Cheeky he would have to solve their new case without him.

"Sorry to give you this one solo, Pal," panted Claude from his prone position, using his trenchcoat as a pillow. "It's not gonna be easy to find out who took Lorena Caldwell's special potion."

"What special potion?" squeaked Cheeky.

"The one she uses to stop crime, end drought, make the sun shine and the flowers grow. It's been missing for at least two weeks."

The last panel showed Cheeky stroking his chin thoughtfully. There were no words. This episode was too serious, and Wendy feared the author of it was trying to send readers a message. She felt queasy, as if she'd eaten something bad.

She'd flipped from Luella's letter immediately to the back page, and so almost missed the front-page story about the new plastics plant. She had heard the rumors, but this was the first story she'd seen about the plant. It was named Planet Friendly Plastics and made outdoor furniture out of recycled plastic. It would employ one hundred people and would hire from all over the region. That was a lot of people for Moffatt Corner.

The story also said the plant would offer higher-than-average wages, according to its owner, Marcinda Adams.

Wendy wondered if the Stiner twins' parents would get jobs there. Sahara and Savannah Stiner had dropped out of extra activities last year to work as checkers at the grocery store. Wendy never saw them anymore unless she went to Otto's Grocery. After school they always had to rush to work.

There were other kids at school whose parents didn't have jobs either, but the Stiners were the only ones Wendy knew personally. Mr. Stiner had worked at the hospital until it closed.

About three months later, Moffatt Corner's veterinarian left town, and Mrs. Stiner, who had been the receptionist, lost her job, too.

Wendy felt lucky that her father had a job, even if he did have to drive to Marlett every day. Terry Wright was the human resources manager for Cole's, the one department store in Marlett.

Before she left for school Monday, Wendy stopped by Miranda's room as always. She stared at her sister's desk for a moment, thinking about what the *Bugle* had meant to Miranda. She was glad her sister wasn't here to see Saturday's paper. Wendy shut the door softly and hurried off.

Libby and Riley were waiting in the usual place. Today Libby wore a lavender suede jumper with a high gathered waistline. The white blouse beneath it had long sleeves that looked as wide as airplane wings. A large bow under her chin made her look like a wrapped present. On her feet were white socks and tennis shoes. She must have brought them to school to change from the Mary Janes her mother usually made her wear.

Wendy tried not to notice the jumper and blouse, but Libby had already seen her looking. "Guess what my mother calls this thing?" She pointed to the jumper.

"A jumper?"

Libby shook her head and looked at Riley. "Don't ask me," he said.

"A pinafore."

"Isn't that just a fancy word for jumper?" asked Wendy.

"I don't know. She could call it a tuxedo, and I'd still look stupid."

Wendy looked down at her own baggy gray sweatpants and sweatshirt, which she hoped hid her extra weight.

"I don't have any room to comment on your clothes," she

said, then changed the subject. "Did you read about the new plant in the *Bugle*? I think it might really help the town." She had decided not to mention the story about the newspaper's bad fortune.

"Yeah," said Riley, "My dad told me about it. He says it's environmentally responsible."

Wendy was about to say something else when Burnam suddenly appeared. "Your stupid paper really blew it this time, Pot!" he yelled, thrusting his angry, thin face inches from hers. He had to stoop his skinny shoulders and bend over to get so close; he had inherited much of his father's height if not his bulk.

Startled, Wendy stepped backward. "What are you talking about?"

"I don't know how it stays in business. And it won't, much longer. It's gonna close even faster than the editor thinks when my father sues it!"

"You don't know everything, Burnam Horton!" snapped Libby.

Wendy looked at her, then at Burnam's surprised face. She knew about Libby's temper, but it was a surprise to most people. Libby kept her innermost thoughts and feelings well-hidden from everyone except her two closest friends. Self-conscious about her clothes, she rarely spoke to anyone besides Wendy and Riley. Now she was actually eye-to-eye with Burnam — she was already tall at five feet, eight inches, and still growing — with her chin thrust out. Even with the big bow jutting out from under her chin, she looked dignified.

"Oh yeah? How about this — my father is the owner of the land that stupid plastics plant is built on. The case is in court, and when he wins, he's going to tear that plant down! And then he's going back to court to sue that stupid paper for printing the story!"

He turned to go, then looked back at Libby and sneered, "What are you wearing tomorrow, a baby bonnet and bib?"

The crowd of boys with him snickered before trotting away, elbowing each other like triumphant football players.

Wendy glanced at Libby, then looked away as her friend's face reddened suddenly. None of them spoke as they turned toward the entrance. Wendy led the way to class. She settled into her desk silently, oblivious to the chatter around her. She was doubtful she'd be able to pay attention to anything. She was wrong.

"I want to talk about the new plastics plant in town," said Mrs. Martino, when she was finished taking roll. "How many of you have heard about it?"

Wendy watched hands go up all over the room before slowly raising her own.

"What do you think that means for a town our size? Good things or bad?" asked Mrs. Martino.

"Good!" exclaimed a short, dark-haired boy near the front of the room. He had just moved to Moffatt Corner this year. His name was Alfred Nava.

"OK, Alfred, suppose you tell us why it's good," said Mrs. Martino.

"My father got a job there as one of the managers," said Alfred. "He says the owner is nice to the workers, and it pays more than the job he had before."

Mrs. Martino nodded. "All right," she said, "so for you it's good personally. Does that mean it's good for the community, too?"

The class was silent. Wendy counted to ten before she slowly raised her hand. She had intended to stay out of the discussion, but she couldn't help it if no one else would say anything.

Mrs. Martino nodded at her and smiled slightly.

"If people can make more money there, then it's good for our overall economy," Wendy said.

"That's stupid!" exploded a voice in the back of the room. She didn't have to look to see who it was. "All it does for the economy is drive up the cost of hiring workers. That means businesses have to pay workers more to compete."

"Who is that bad for?" asked Alfred. "It means that the workers will have more money to buy things from those businesses. So it should help."

"Yeah," said another student, a girl named Morgan Mitchell. "And it means that more people can get jobs. There isn't enough work here for everyone who wants to work."

The class was silent as students looked at each other. Most students never contradicted Burnam Horton, but neither Alfred nor Morgan would know that since they were new students.

"It looks as if we have two competing points of view," said Mrs. Martino. "Does anyone want to expand on either one of them?"

"If businesses have to pay more money to hire people, they might just decide to move out of town and go somewhere else!" said Burnam. "Maybe that will teach a lesson to all these greedy people who want more money."

Mrs. Martino looked at the class for a response. At first, no one spoke although several people appeared on the verge of it. Finally, Wendy couldn't take the silence any more. She knew if she didn't say what she was thinking, she'd be mad at herself the rest of the day.

"I don't know why it's considered greedy to want more money for your family," she said. "Isn't that what everyone wants?" She turned and looked right at Burnam, whose dark eyes bored into her. She knew he was trying to scare her, and she struggled to keep her voice steady. "I know of kids our age who have had to go to work because their parents lost their jobs here and couldn't find anywhere else to work. If the new plant can give their parents jobs, then it should help more than it hurts. Shouldn't it?"

A few heads nodded, but no one else spoke. Burnam continued to stare at her. Wendy turned away from him and glanced at Mrs. Martino, who smiled.

"I think this has been a good lesson in civics," she said. "In a democracy, there are always competing economic interests. Competition is supposed to make us strong. For Friday's class, I want you all to write two hundred words on whether a new business might hurt or help a small town. There is no wrong or right point of view, but I do expect you to support your opinion with sound reasons."

There were groans all around. Then Burnam asked, "Could we write our essays about a business that's already here?"

Mrs. Martino looked at him for a moment. "What business did you have in mind?"

"The *Bugle*," he said. "I think it's harmful to the town. It prints half-baked stories and opinions instead of news."

"What reasoning would you use to back that up?"

The class was so silent you could hear people breathing. Wendy sneaked a glance at Burnam. His face was red and his lips were curled in a sneer. "I think, Burnam, that the class should do the same assignment," said Mrs. Martino.

He didn't say anything, but Wendy's insides told her this wasn't over. And she was right. When Mrs. Martino asked on Friday who wanted to read his essay, Burnam waved his hand. "All right," said Mrs. Martino. "Come to the front of the class, please, and read it."

He started out by reading the title, "Why the New Plastics

Plant is Bad for Moffatt Corner," which told Wendy that he was cheating by using the title as part of his word count. He used the same argument about paying workers that he had offered in class. Wendy stole a look at Mrs. Martino, who stood to one side of Burnam, her face expressionless, looking at the class as he read.

Then he read, "Another business that is bad for Moffatt Corner is the *Bugle*, the so-called town newspaper that reports lies and half-truth as fact. It will close soon because of one of these lies, and the residents of town will not have to put up with it any longer. This will be for the better. The end."

He tapped the edge of the papers on Mrs. Martino's desk and smiled triumphantly at the class. Snickers erupted from the back of the room. Wide-eyed, Wendy looked again at Mrs. Martino to see what she would do. "Thank you, Burnam. Alfred, would you care to read your essay?"

He began reading, but Wendy barely heard any of the words. She was stuck on what Burnam had gotten away with. Alfred sat down and a couple more people got up to read their essays. Then it was almost time for the bell, so Mrs. Martino had students pass their essays to the front. "You will get them back with grades next week," she said. "Oh, and—" the bell rang shrilly, interrupting her. As soon as it was silent, she said as students were filing out, "Burnam, stay just a moment, please."

Wendy sucked in her breath and tried to linger and eavesdrop, but she was blocking several students' path to the door. She had to satisfy herself with a backward glance at Burnam trudging slowly up to the teacher's desk as Mrs. Martino watched him with the same expressionless look.

—— Four ——

'Bugle' Seeks New Owner

"Mom, where's the *Bugle*?" Wendy called. It was Saturday morning, laundry day, and from her spot in the kitchen, Wendy could see her mother in the laundry room, loading clothes in the washing machine.

Her father sometimes worked on Saturdays, but he always left the newspaper on the kitchen table. It wasn't there. It wasn't next to his recliner in the den, either.

Wendy's mother came into the kitchen without answering and headed for the stove. The kitchen smelled wonderful, a combination of bread baking and other odors Wendy couldn't identify. Her mouth watered.

Wanda Wright looked neat and trim in beige slacks and sweater. Her brown hair was pulled back and knotted into a twist low on her neck. Wendy bet other mothers didn't look that good on Saturday morning. She looked down at her own thick torso. She would never look as good as her mom, not even when she was thirty-five.

She and Miranda had talked often about how pretty their mother was.

"You look like her, you know," Miranda always said.

"You have her eyes," Wendy would reply.

"You have her smile, her hair and her shape," Miranda would say, adding before Wendy could protest, "and don't talk to me about being overweight. It's just baby fat. Underneath, you have her shape." That usually ended the conversation. For several reasons, Wendy didn't like to talk about body shapes with Miranda, although she realized much later, after Miranda was gone, that it would have been OK. Miranda would have talked about anything, even things she didn't have.

Back then, Wendy felt closer to having her mother's shape than she did now. That was before she had to eat everything Wanda cooked so she wouldn't hurt her feelings. Back then, Wanda hadn't cooked so much, and life seemed normal, even though Miranda wasn't like other people.

Wendy's sister had been born with arms she couldn't use. They hung unmoving from her shoulders. Just below her waistline, attached to the arms, were hands that curled up like claws.

Miranda could walk fine and had trained herself to use her mouth and her feet to do things her hands couldn't. She could hold a fork with her toes. And she could write by holding a pen in her mouth.

"Mom, do you know where the paper is?" Wendy asked again.

Her mother didn't turn around. She was making Hollandaise sauce for Eggs Benedict, and the mixture required constant stirring.

"Would you like orange juice or apple juice, Wendy?" she asked.

"Either. Well, do you? Know where the paper is?" Wendy

drummed her fingers on the table.

"Your father had it earlier."

"But it's not here! He always leaves it right here!" Wendy stared at the neat hair. Her mother was stalling.

After another pause, her mother's beige shoulders sagged slightly and she let out a short sigh. She opened the cabinet door under the kitchen sink and fished the newspaper from the trash can, brushing off wet coffee grounds and egg shells.

"I threw it out," she said, handing the soiled, wet paper to Wendy without apology. "I hoped if it was gone you wouldn't notice. Silly me."

Frowning, Wendy took the paper. Her mother didn't care about the *Bugle*, but she had never just tossed it before. Why today?

She didn't wonder long. She quickly spotted the story in the lower right-hand corner of the front page. This headline said " 'Bugle' to close if buyer isn't found."

This time the information was a story instead of a letter. It said Luella Cathcart was now searching for someone to buy the paper. If no one did, the paper would have to close in a month. The story said she thanked readers for their interest and support over the years, as if it were stopping publication right away, and ended without saying anything else.

"Now you know," her mother said, placing a plate with fresh, buttered bread and Eggs Benedict slathered with Hollandaise in front of Wendy. It was garnished with a sliver of parsley. Wendy stared at the tiny, dark green stalk and wondered what her mother would say if she ate only that.

"The other day the editor said she had done some things she hoped would fix the paper's problems," Wendy said with a sigh.

"Maybe the situation was worse than she originally

thought," said her mother.

"I'm not hungry," Wendy said.

"I was afraid of just that happening. Now what am I supposed to do with this food?"

"I don't know. Save it for lunch."

"It will taste awful then. You can't reheat Eggs Benedict in the microwave. Wendy, I'm sorry about the paper. But it can't be your life. Eat."

Wendy didn't hear her. She was thinking about Luella Cathcart. She had first talked to the editor when she was eight. Wendy had mailed in one of Miranda's essays. She hadn't asked her sister first. It was the only time she ever took something of Miranda's without her permission. She knew it would be all right, though. Miranda had once told her that getting something published in the *Bugle* would be "the apex."

The essay was about a busy squirrel Miranda had watched from her window on a day she was sick in bed. Wendy had read her sister's poetry for years and pretended to like it even though she didn't understand it. The squirrel story she understood. She mailed it off to Luella Cathcart. The editor had called the Wright house a few days later and asked for Wendy, since her name was on the return address.

"Wendy Wright?" the editor had demanded. "Are you the one who sent me the squirrel story?"

"Yes. My sister wrote it."

"How come she didn't send it to me?"

"I dunno," lied Wendy.

"You want me to publish it, don't you? If I'm going to publish it, I need her permission."

"You're going to put it in the paper?"

"That's what I said, isn't it? I need her permission. I'd also like her to write one for every issue. You can tell her I'll pay her five dollars a column."

Wendy hadn't known what to say, so she didn't say anything.

"Are you there? Do I have her permission or not?"

"Sure."

"And you'll tell her about writing more? I thought we could call the column 'My Window.' If she wants another name on it, we can talk. But it'd have to be awfully good to make me change my mind."

"OK."

"I don't want any trouble over this. I think I should talk to her."

"She's not here right now," fibbed Wendy. She could tell that Luella was suspicious, but the editor had finally hung up after getting the correct spelling of Miranda's name. Wendy had waited until the next *Bugle* came out to tell Miranda about the column, just to make sure the editor was going to do what she said.

Miranda's eyes were round and big and shiny as new nickels when she saw her column in the paper. Then Wendy told her about writing another one for every issue of the *Bugle*.

"See, it says so right here at the bottom of the squirrel story: 'Miranda Wright, a new columnist for the *Bugle*, will write 'My Window' twice a week beginning today.' Isn't that great?"

"But what will I write about twice a week?" Miranda had asked. "What if that was the only story I had in me?"

"How'd you get that story?"

"By staring out the window."

"Maybe if you stared out the window some more, you'd get another story."

To anyone else, it would have sounded lame, but not to Miranda. She had an active mind and could have created a story about a pebble. She began staring out the window all the time, and from that week on, "My Window" appeared in the *Bugle*, carefully proofread first by Wendy, who would look up words she didn't understand. Miranda would never send out a column that Wendy hadn't proofread first, even when she was right on deadline.

Then one of Luella's reporters came to do a story about Miranda, and called her "at fifteen, the youngest columnist the *Bugle* had carried, and maybe the youngest newspaper columnist in the country." She also wrote that Miranda had started reading the *Bugle* when she was ten and had not missed an issue since. Luella didn't believe that, so she called to check.

Miranda said it was true, so Luella gave her a free subscription in addition to the five dollars a column. And a picture of Miranda started running with the column.

Miranda died in her sleep four years after "My Window" started. She had already written her column for the next issue, and Wendy delivered it to the *Bugle* in person because she wanted to make sure it was published, and no one else in her family would have thought about it. The *Bugle* put the column with her obituary on the front page. It noted that she had written almost four hundred columns.

In the space where "My Window" usually was on page two, Luella left a blank space except for the words, "In Memory of Miranda Wright" for four issues.

Soon Miranda's free subscription stopped. Wendy hadn't seen Luella Cathcart since she delivered that final column. But she still read the paper every day, and still thought of the *Bugle* as Miranda's paper.

"The *Bugle* has to keep printing," she said, half to herself, as her mother scraped Eggs Benedict into the garbage disposal. "Miranda wouldn't want it to close."

Her mother didn't answer. Wanda never talked about Miranda, not once since her funeral.

When her mother left to buy groceries, Wendy didn't know what to do, but she knew she had to talk to someone. She grabbed the phone and dialed Riley's number. His mother answered.

"Oh, I'm sorry, Wendy, but he's gone fishing with his father. I don't expect them back until late tonight."

"If he doesn't get in too late, could you ask him to call me?" Wendy asked, trying to keep the disappointment out of her voice. She put down the receiver and stood there, her hand still on the phone.

Libby had gone out of town for the weekend with her mother, to visit an aunt. Wanda would be gone for a couple of hours. She could stay home alone and mope. Or she could go somewhere herself.

She grabbed the notepad near the phone, scribbled a note to her mother — "Riding my bike. Be back soon" — then took off toward downtown, pedaling toward the *Bugle* office on Main Street. She didn't know what she'd do when she got there, but maybe something would come to her.

Ten minutes later, she stood outside the *Bugle* building, or One Bugle Square, as a big white sign with black letters called it. The sign was new and was like one you would see on a large building in the middle of a big city. It looked out of place here, on the old-fashioned *Bugle* office, in the middle of other old store fronts. She wondered what had made Luella Cathcart think to put up a sign like that.

She tried the front door, but it was locked. She peered into the dingy front window. No one appeared to be inside. She should have known the office would be closed on Saturday.

As she sat on the sidewalk in front of the office, watching

31

the cars on Main and trying to figure out what to do, a car pulled up to the three news racks outside the convenience store across the street, and a woman got out to look at them. The *Bugle*'s rack was on her left, the first of the three. The driver studied all three front pages, then selected the *Marlett Muse* from the center news rack.

"Hey!" Wendy yelled. "You should get the local paper! Where's your loyalty?"

The woman scowled at Wendy, got back into her car, and drove off. Wendy couldn't really blame her for buying the Marlett paper. The *Muse* was a daily, and anyway, it seemed like everybody shopped in Marlett these days. It had more than four times Moffatt Corner's population and three grocery stores to choose from. More people from Moffatt Corner were going to doctors there, too, since the local hospital closed.

But the thirty miles of road from Moffatt Corner to Marlett had become the busiest when the Marlett Mall opened two years ago. Moffatt Corner was supposed to get that mall.

The *Bugle* had reported that the mall was going to be built at the edge of town as soon as developers could buy land. A later story said they were dealing with a property owner. The paper carried no more stories about the mall for months after that, until a story appeared saying that land would be broken the following week for the Marlett Mall. Officials said they were unable to find a good location in Moffatt Corner.

Everybody knew that was the cleaned-up version of the story. The real story was that the person who owned the land had been told by the mayor that he shouldn't sell, especially if he wanted to keep his garbage collection contract with the city. The mayor had gotten his instructions from someone who owned a store in Moffatt Corner, someone who didn't want competition from stores in the mall. Everyone knew who made the threat, too.

Wendy headed for home, pedaling past the hospital. Boards were nailed across the front windows, which someone had shattered months ago. She went past Otto's, the only grocery store still open. Three cars were in the parking lot, and one of them was the owner's. Even her mother went to Marlett for groceries when she needed more than a few things. She said it was cheaper.

She pedaled furiously, her feet moving so fast that the right one slipped off the pedal, which whirled around and cracked her in the shin. "Ouch!" she cried, stopping her bike to rub her bruised leg. But the pain that hurt worse was in her head. Thinking Miranda's *Bugle* might close gave her such a headache she couldn't see straight.

—— Five ——

The Girl Scout Cookie Fib

Monday morning at school Wendy looked in all directions for Libby and Riley. But the person she saw first was Burnam.

"Did you see the story, Pot? The *Bugle*'s going to close unless someone buys it and keeps it open! And my dad says nobody's going to buy that piece of junk. He said it doesn't matter who owns it, it's still going to have money problems. He'll see to it."

He smirked and thrust out his chin, waiting for her to say something. She clamped her teeth firmly on her tongue to keep silent.

"You know what else? He didn't even have to sue. He just decided not to advertise. And if that's not enough to close the place down, he knows some other people who will quit advertising, too."

Wendy bit her tongue until it hurt, but she couldn't be silent any longer. "He didn't sue because there was nothing to sue for, and you know it!" she yelled. "Everyone in town knows what's going on. Anyway," she said, trying to be calm, "the *Bugle* isn't going to close." She hoped she sounded more confident than she felt. Her neck was hot and sweaty. "By the way," she said in her most casual voice, "what grade did Mrs. Martino give you on your essay?"

His smirk faded and his face turned a faint pink. "The same grade everyone else got on that bogus assignment!" he snapped.

"Oh? I got an A. So you got an A too?"

He backed away from her. "Teacher's pet!" he yelled. "You should mind your own beeswax!"

She watched him with a small smile on her face. It felt good for once to see Burnam uncomfortable over something she'd said, instead of the other way around. She had no way of knowing what Burnam got on the essay, but she'd bet her life it was a D or F. That's what Mrs. Martino gave people who didn't follow instructions.

As Libby and Riley walked up, Burnam looked Libby up and down, staring at her overalls and puffy-sleeved blouse. But he didn't say anything before stomping off.

"He looked really mad," said Libby. "What did you say to him?"

"I don't want to talk about him. He's always mad," she said, shaking her head. "Where have you two been, anyway? I need to talk to you about something, and we don't have much time before first period. You two meet me here right after last period. We have to go somewhere."

"But I can't," Libby said. "I have ballet right after school."

"You can do ballet anytime. This is important."

Libby opened her mouth to argue, then saw the set of Wendy's jaw. She sighed and then nodded. Wendy turned to look at Riley. He shrugged. "I wasn't going anywhere but home, and no one else will be there until about five-thirty. So I guess I'm in. Where are we going?"

"To the *Bugle* office."

"But – "Libby began.

"Why?" asked Riley.

Both were cut off by the ringing school bell, and they were talking to thin air anyway. Wendy had already loped off.

At three that afternoon, the trio sat on three dented, faded green metal folding chairs against a wall in the dingy *Bugle* newsroom. The receptionist had called this the waiting area.

"We were going to practice jetes today, you know," whined Libby. "Everyone will be ahead of me now. I probably won't get picked for the ballet recital, and Mom will be furious."

She was perched on the edge of her chair. Riley sat between her and Wendy.

Libby hadn't mentioned ballet again until now. Even so, Wendy knew she was upset about missing class. Not because she liked ballet or wanted to be in the recital — she hated both the class and recitals. But she didn't want to make her mother mad.

"I'll practice jetes with you later, OK? It's just some kind of jump. We'll rent a video and practice together," said Wendy.

"I've never seen a ballet video," replied Libby, sticking her legs out in front of her and leaning forward from her waist as far as she could go. Ever since she started ballet, she stretched all the time. It irritated Wendy, mostly because she was jealous at how limber Libby was. "I bet you haven't ever seen one, either," continued Libby. "How come your mother didn't pick you up after school?"

"She had to go to a meeting. She asked our neighbor to pick me up."

"That woman in the blue car?" Riley asked. "So what did you tell her?"

"That my mom forgot I had band practice, and I'd get a ride home later."

"But you aren't in band," said Libby.

"So? You aren't either," retorted Wendy.

"That isn't the point," said Riley, who never lost sight of the point. "What are you going to do when your neighbor tells your mom that you stayed late for band practice?"

"I'll handle that if it comes up."

"It may come up, if we have to wait here much longer," he said. "I can imagine your mother wondering at nine o'clock tonight where you are, and she calls the neighbor who tells her you stayed after school to practice with the band. And your mother is wondering what band and sends out the police to find you."

"Nine o'clock!" wailed Libby. "I can't be here until nine o'clock! My mother would send out the National Guard!"

"None of us can be here that late, silly!" snapped Wendy. "Riley, would you just hush up? If we ever get to see the editor" — she glanced at the receptionist, who was typing with great speed — "we won't be here that long."

"What's this 'we' business?" asked Libby. "I don't believe I want to see the editor. What would I say to him?"

"Her. The editor is a her," corrected Wendy. "Which you would know if you'd read her stories about the *Bugle* being in trouble. Anyway, you don't need to say anything. I'll do the talking."

"If you're going to do the talking, why do we even have to be here?" Libby asked. "Anyway, didn't you tell me you met her once?"

"That was two years ago, Libby. I look different now. She won't remember me."

She sighed, wondering why she thought it was a good idea to bring them. They had whined and argued since school let out. Then she reminded herself she needed them if her plan was going to work.

Tired of waiting, she walked to the receptionist's desk. "Excuse me, but I think we've been sitting here an hour. "

The receptionist glanced at her wall clock. "You've been here twenty minutes. I buzzed Ms. Cathcart, but maybe she forgot. I'll go see. What did you say you wanted?"

"I want to sell her some Girl Scout cookies," said Wendy.

The receptionist regarded her for a moment. Wendy gave her a toothy grin. The receptionist looked about the same age as Wendy's mother, and wore her dark brown hair short and curly. She was dressed neatly in trim black pants and a red knit top.

"Do you write for the paper?" Wendy asked.

"Sometimes," the woman said. "I usually do other things, but I may be doing more reporting now, since the layoff." She shifted in her chair and got up. "I'll be right back."

She walked past Libby and Riley, down a long hall. Wendy watched her as she tapped on the last door on the left, listened for a moment, then went in. After what seemed like another hour but was really just a few minutes, she came out and motioned to them.

"You can go in now," she said. "But I warn you, she isn't in a very good mood. So don't expect her to buy many Girl Scout cookies."

"You said we were here to sell Girl Scout cookies?" whispered Riley. "Did it ever occur to you that someone might not like you lying to get in to see them?"

"I can't believe you got me into this," moaned Libby.

"Be quiet, both of you!" hissed Wendy. "Let's go in before she changes her mind."

"No thanks," said Riley. "You can just go in there by yourself. I'll wait here."

"Me, too," said Libby.

Wendy started to argue, but the receptionist was staring. With just one buzz of the phone, she could lock the editor's door to them forever.

"Fine. Just stay here then!" Wendy turned, walked down the hall and put her hand on the doorknob, trying not to think about what she would say or do. She rapped lightly on the door, heard no answer and rapped again. Then she heard a hoarse voice: "Door's not locked."

Luella Cathcart's office smelled of coffee and cigarettes, odors Wendy remembered from her last visit. Late afternoon light streamed in from the streaky, bare windows, and stacks of newspapers three feet and higher lined three walls. On one side of the office was a table of trophies. The inscription on one said "Best news story in a non-daily paper." Another read "First Place — Photography."

On several of the walls were yellowed front pages of the *Bugle*, in scuffed brown frames. Most of them hung crooked.

"Didn't you bring any cookies with you for me to sample?" rasped Luella Cathcart, who sat behind a massive brown desk. "I could use a snack."

Wendy stared mutely at her. She looked about the same as she had the last time. Her short white hair was whiter and standing up in places, as if she had clawed through it recently. Even though she was sitting, you could tell she was short and square from the shape of her shoulders. She wore a black sweatshirt and jeans.

"Well?" she barked. "Where are the cookies?"

"I don't have any. I forgot them."

"How could a Girl Scout forget her cookies? That would get you kicked out of Girl Scouts in my day!"

"You were a Girl Scout?" croaked Wendy.

"Never mind! Give me the order form. You can deliver them

later."

"I don't have that, either. I…I forgot that, too."

The editor stared at her, and Wendy knew she was caught.

"Don't I know you from somewhere? What's your name?" demanded Luella.

Wendy opened her mouth, but nothing came out. She was taller than the last time she saw Luella, and probably fatter, too. She truly had not thought the editor would recognize her. Luella drummed her fingers on the desk.

"I, uh, have a question. I just wondered if it was true that one person could make the *Bugle* close."

"What's your name?" demanded Luella again. "I may forget a face, but never a name."

"My name is Wendy Wright."

The editor still stared. "Is that a made-up name? Did Horton send you over here to spy on me? I bet you're one of his kids, aren't you? Or he's paying you. That's pretty low, using a kid to spy for you. You can just tell him —"

"No!" cried Wendy, shaking her head wildly. "I am really Wendy Wright. Mr. Horton only has a son, I think. We're not even friends. I'm not a spy, I'm…" she stopped short. She had been about to say that she was the sister of Miranda Wright, although she hadn't wanted to bring that up yet.

"Wendy Wright…" said the editor. "Now I remember. Your sister wrote a column for us. You sent me the very first one. Then your sister ummm…" Luella suddenly got busy shuffling papers on her desk. "You should have said who you were! I really don't have time for this. So unless you can tell me why you are here…"

"I already told you. I want to know if it's true the *Bugle* is going to close. I don't want it to close. Moffatt Corner needs a newspaper."

"You read the paper? Most of the time I wonder if anybody does." Luella stuck a cigarette in her mouth, then pulled it out and stared at it. "Yes," she said, her voice faded. "It looks like it will close."

"Is it true one person has enough power to close it? And why does Mr. Horton hate the *Bugle* so much?"

Luella put the cigarette back in her mouth and lighted it, staring again at Wendy. Smoke snaked its way to Wendy's eyes, and she waved it away.

"Yes to your first question, especially in a town this size, and it's too complicated to talk about your second. I've got something somewhere..." She put the cigarette down on the edge of her desk and rummaged in the top right-hand drawer. Wendy watched the ash grow longer and longer, as Luella Cathcart continued to dig in the drawer.

Just as the ash was about to drop into the drawer full of papers, the editor picked up the cigarette, flicked the ash onto the floor and put the cigarette in the corner of her mouth. "Here," she said, thrusting several yellowed clippings in Wendy's hands. "This explains some things. Take them and go. I have things to do. But be sure you bring all those stories back!"

Wendy obeyed, hurrying out the door. At least she had an invitation to return. Libby and Riley were waiting.

"What happened?" asked Riley.

"I found out some of what I wanted to know," said Wendy. That was enough for now.

——— Six ———

Stop the Presses!

Once again, "Cheeky and Claude" wasn't funny. It started out with Cheeky reading facts from his notepad to Claude. "Lorena Caldwell last saw her special potion nine days ago. It was in a bright blue bottle decorated with silver stars and a moon, and it had a cork stopper."

Claude, still prone, lifted his head slightly and shifted his ears forward. "Who was in the herbal shop that day?"

"The postman. A woman buying herbal hand lotion. Mrs. Irwin came in to get her special skin soap. And a man no one seems to remember anything about."

"What do they say about him?" asked Claude, his head higher this time. The strip ended there, before telling anyone Cheeky's answer. So you were left wondering who the man was, or at least what he looked like.

The comic strip was the subject of Wendy's first class. Mrs. Martino had clipped out the strip and tacked it to the bulletin board when the mystery first started. This morning she told her students to take a few minutes and read the strip. Wendy looked around as everyone crowded at the front of the room. Only she and Burnam didn't go. "I assume you two have read the strip today?" Mrs. Martino said. Wendy nodded.

"I'll read it later," said Burnam, indifferently.

"We may discuss it in class," said Mrs. Martino. "Please read it now."

Burnam opened his mouth as if to argue but said nothing. Refusing to look at the teacher, he dragged his feet all the way to the bulletin board and glanced at the comic strip for less than a minute before going back to his desk. The class had a lively discussion about who the mystery man was before turning to other topics. Burnam didn't participate.

At lunch that day, Wendy told Libby and Riley about the *Bugle* editor's suspicions that she was a spy.

"A spy?" Libby's eyes were round. "Why'd she think that?"

"I don't know. Maybe she suspects everyone."

"Couldn't she do anything that would keep people's ads in the paper?" asked Libby.

"Sure," said Wendy, looking around to make sure no one was eavesdropping this time. "She could have done what Mr. Horton told her to do, and not printed the story about the plastics plant. But then the *Bugle* wouldn't be a very good newspaper, would it?"

Then she told them that Luella had recognized her after all, and had loaned her some old newspaper clippings. When she first looked at the old stories, she wondered how she had missed the story. Then she saw the date; the story had been printed almost ten years ago, when she was only four. It told the tale of the feud between Mr. Horton and Marcinda Adams, who owned the plastics plant and the land it was on. Burnam Horton Sr. had taken Adams to court, insisting the land was his, even though his father had sold it to Marcinda Adams' grandfather almost fifty years ago.

The courts couldn't rule against legal deeds, so next Mr. Horton tried to fight the zoning for the plastics plant. The problem with that was the land had always been zoned industrial. Once he found he couldn't overturn the zoning, he started a political campaign, holding press conferences which criticized the "interlopers" who would foul Moffatt Corner's air and water with their business. Of course, Luella Cathcart always printed Marcinda Adams' responses to his charges, and Ms. Adams pointed out that her industry was clean and would not foul anything.

Then Mr. Horton's press conferences began to target the local newspaper, and Luella covered those, too. He would say things like "Don't buy into newspaper stories that publish only half-truths!" Luella would ask him what was not true, and he would answer "Don't YOU know? You wrote it!"

"So why was he so against the plastics plant?" asked Libby. "And why did it take so long to build it and get it going?"

"I'll have to ask Ms. Cathcart, but it's probably just what Burnam said the other day in class about new businesses making wages more competitive so that employers had to pay more to keep their employees. And it took so long to build the plant because Mr. Horton fought everything in court, from the building permits to the number of fire control sprinklers installed to the landscaping."

Libby sighed. "It sounds like the *Bugle* could have avoided the fight if the editor had just ignored the whole story and covered something else. That's what she should have done."

Wendy started to argue but Riley spoke up first. "Remember last year when you worked on the yearbook and those two cheerleaders were always fighting about something? What if Mindy Waller had threatened to get her parents to pull their restaurant ad from the back of the yearbook unless you left out Carmen Brownfield's picture?"

"That would be silly, Riley. It's not like leaving out Carmen's picture would mean that she wasn't a cheerleader. Everyone would know the picture was supposed to be there and wonder why it wasn't. Besides, it wouldn't be fair to Carmen."

"So what would you have told Mindy if she said you should leave it out?" he persisted.

"I guess I'd have told her I was sorry, but Carmen's picture would be in the yearbook along with everyone else's."

"And if the Wallers canceled their ad?"

"We'd make the yearbook money up, I guess." She shrugged. "But it isn't the same thing as the *Bugle* not running a story. When the editor decided to run that story, people at the *Bugle* lost their jobs. That's not fair to them."

"So if you were the editor, you would have done what Mr. Horton told you to do?"

Libby looked down at her hands, which rested gracefully in her lap. She looked pale, the way she always did when someone argued with her. But she thought about it awhile before answering, and came up with the answer Wendy was expecting. "I guess not," she mumbled, her face turning red. "It would be easier, but it wouldn't be right. And everybody would know that I caved in and ignored the real news."

They were all quiet for a moment, knowing Libby was embarrassed but not knowing how to fix it. Then Riley looked at Wendy expectantly. "Well? Are you going to ask us something?"

She nodded, smiling. Riley could read her mind. "Yes. Can you go back to the *Bugle* with me today?"

"Why?"

"To get jobs there."

"Why would the editor hire us?" he asked. "I don't know how to do anything there. Do you?"

Wendy nodded. "I have experience in proofreading. And I bet I could do other things."

"It sounds pretty crazy to me. And even if there is something we could do, how are you going to convince the editor?"

Wendy had no answer. She knew it sounded crazy. But she also knew she had to try.

"I'll go with you, Wendy," murmured Libby.

Wendy smiled at her, reached over and squeezed her arm. She knew Libby would come through. "Thanks. You know you'll have to miss ballet. And sometimes people get mad at you about what's in the paper. Even things you didn't have anything to do with."

"Missing ballet is a good reason to do it."

"What will you tell your mother?"

Libby shrugged. "What will you tell yours?"

"I don't know yet either."

They both looked at Riley. "Oh, OK, I'll go. But I bet she kicks us out of her office."

Wendy called her mother from school and said she was going to Libby's house. Libby didn't tell her mother anything, since she was supposed to be at ballet.

Once they arrived at the *Bugle* office, it appeared they wouldn't be able to see the editor.

"I don't think she has time," the receptionist said, frowning as they walked up to her desk.

"We've come to help," Wendy said.

"Help with what?"

"The paper. You don't have enough employees. We'll work for free. Maybe then she won't have to sell it. Or close it."

Arms folded across her chest, the receptionist asked, "How

long do you think that would actually help?"

Wendy shrugged, suddenly unsure of herself. She looked down at the receptionist's desk, tracing an imaginary pattern with her finger. "Maybe if we can write more stories, you won't have to put things in the paper that nobody wants to read. And then more people will read it."

The receptionist stared at them, arms still crossed, and raised her eyebrows. Wendy braced herself to hear, "Get out!" and backed up when the receptionist stood. Without a word, she turned and walked down the hall. She looked back at the three of them staring at her. "Follow me," she commanded, and they obeyed. She stopped at the last door on the left and rapped.

"What is it now?" growled a voice. Wendy glanced at Libby, who looked pale.

"Somebody to see you," said the receptionist as she opened the door. "Three somebodies."

She turned, pressing her back into the editor's door and motioning the trio inside. Wendy went through first, stumbling and almost falling, then Riley followed. Libby came in last, face pink. The receptionist nudged her slightly to hurry her along, then stood behind them.

"Oh for the love of...now what do you want? Tina! Don't just stand there – take these kids out! What do I pay you for?"

"You haven't paid me in weeks, Luella. You need to hear what they have to say."

The editor glared at her, then at Wendy. "No more cookie stories!"

"No ma'am, and here are your clippings." She hastily plopped them on Luella's desk then backed up. "I want to introduce my friends, Riley Davis and Libby Weaver," she said, her face red.

The editor glanced from Wendy to the other two, staring

briefly at the big ruffle around Libby's neck. "Fine. Tina says I have to listen and she's the boss," she said, glaring at the receptionist again. "What do you want?"

"We're here to help," said Wendy. She had meant to prepare a better opening, but hadn't been able to think of anything else.

The silence seemed unending. Wendy could tell without looking that neither Riley nor Libby was breathing. She kept her eyes on Luella Cathcart's face. The editor's expression never changed, but her eyes skipped over their three faces, to Riley's hair, then again to the ruffle that encased Libby's neck, then to Tina.

"OK," she rasped, glaring at Wendy. "Can any of you type?"

Wendy glanced at Riley, who shook his head, then at Libby, whom she knew could type. But Libby kept her eyes glued to the floor. She was too afraid to speak.

"Can you cover a meeting? Take a picture? Deliver papers?"

Wendy chewed on her lip. "We might could deliver papers," she said.

"Oh. You can drive a car then."

"No, but we all have bicycles."

"You know how long it would take you on a bike?" demanded Luella.

"Not that long, with our circulation," offered Tina.

Her eyes blazing, Luella glared at her before continuing. "And when would you deliver it? I can just see you, trying to find the right addresses, wheeling around town on your bikes in the dark. What would your parents think about that?"

Nobody dared answer.

"I know!" she cried, pointing at Libby's ruffles. "You could cover fashion for me!"

Wendy could feel her anger heating up the roots of her hair.

She felt as hot as she did during the summer when she mowed the grass, and if she'd seen herself in a mirror, she would have noticed only the angry red in her face, which overpowered everything else.

"Stop it!" she cried. "Don't make fun of us. We came here to help, and you think it's a big joke. Maybe you don't deserve the *Bugle*, if you think everything's such a joke!"

The editor's mouth gaped, but Libby piped up before she could respond.

"I can type. I can type fifty words a minute. I'd get faster if I did it every day."

"And I can deliver papers on my bike," said Riley. "I'm fast, probably as fast as anyone who delivers them in a car. I could set up a system, maybe get others to help me. Maybe you could start your press earlier and we could get started earlier, and then we wouldn't have to deliver papers in the dark. Like Tina says, how many could there be?"

The editor propped up her head on stubby fingers, her lower lip stuck out. Her other hand twiddled with a cigarette. Without moving her head, she eyed them one at a time. "I don't need anyone to deliver papers or type, although that is a wonderful skill," she said, rolling her eyes. "What I need, you kids can't give me."

"What?" asked Wendy.

"Money."

"Which you get from ads, right?" asked Riley.

"Bingo!" she said.

"We can sell ads. We sell all sorts of things at school — coupon books, candy, wrapping paper. How is selling an ad different? It should be easier!"

The editor looked at him, then back at Tina. "You got me into this," she began.

"What could it hurt?" asked Tina, shrugging. "You might even get to keep the *Bugle* an extra month."

Luella shook her head and let out a deep sigh. "I am losing my mind," she said. "All right," she said looking at Tina. "You let them in here — you handle it! Close the door behind you!" She looked at Tina as if she expected an argument. Instead, the receptionist motioned for the three to follow her. Back at her desk, she rummaged through papers. She found the one she was looking for, a small scrap with one torn edge, and handed it to Wendy.

"This guy just opened a shop. He sells skates and stuff. See if you can sell him an ad. If you don't sell the ad, don't come back. Just call me."

"But that's not much of a chance," protested Wendy. "What about Libby typing, and Riley delivering papers?"

"What we need right now is money. Cash. A check is fine, but don't let him try to pay you after the ad is published." She held up her hands as Wendy began to protest again. "This is your only shot. Let me know something by tomorrow." She turned back to her typing.

Wendy led the way out, looking back only once. Outside, the trio stared at each other.

"Guess we'd better get started," said Riley. "We don't have much time."

"Since when have you been a salesman?" Wendy asked Riley.

"Since third grade. I guess you could call me a veteran. People see me coming with a coupon book and cover their wallets with their hands. It doesn't do any good, though. I can talk people into anything."

"Good," said Wendy. "Then you'll know what to say to this skate shop guy."

—— Seven——

A Sales Job

None of them had thought to look at the name on the scrap of paper. Wendy pulled it out of her pocket and read it.

"What's it say?" Riley asked.

"It's just a name and a phone number. Nothing else. We need to find a phone."

Myra's House of Beauty hair salon was across the street.

"We can go over there and ask to use the phone," said Wendy, "or we can go back to the *Bugle* and see if Tina would let us use her phone."

"I don't want to go back just now," said Riley.

"Me neither," said Libby.

"OK. It's Myra's, I guess," said Wendy. "Who is going to call?"

Libby looked at her feet, and Riley scratched his head. "I guess I have the most sales experience," he said. "But I don't want to go into Myra's. It's all women, I bet, and they'd stare at me."

"Maybe we should practice on each other, and whoever sounds

the best could call," offered Libby.

They agreed it was a good idea, and Wendy volunteered to go first, with Riley being the person she was trying to sell an ad to.

"Your name is Paul Calhoun," said Wendy, reading from the scrap of paper. She pretended to punch in numbers on a telephone. "It's ringing," she told Riley.

"Hello, this is Paul Calhoun. May I help you?"

"Yes. This is Wendy Wright from the *Bugle*, and I was wondering —"

"*Bugle*? What's the *Bugle*?"

"It's the newspaper here in Moffatt Corner, the only local paper in town. It comes out twice a week, on Wednesdays and Saturdays. May I bring an issue by to show you?"

"Oh, I wouldn't have time for that. I'm very busy today."

Wendy hesitated, thinking. "Could I have your address anyway? I'd like to come by and see your store."

"We're not open yet. We will be in about three weeks."

"Eat roaches, Riley!" snapped Wendy. "Think you could make this a little harder? Why don't you just tell me I have the wrong number while you're at it?"

"I'm sorry, you have the wrong number. Click." Riley moved his hand as if he were hanging up a phone.

"What are you trying to do?" Wendy demanded, glaring.

"Any of that could happen," Riley said, pushing up his glasses, which immediately slipped down to the tip of his nose again. "You need to be prepared."

Before Wendy could say anything else, Libby stepped between them. "You should just go ahead and call, Wendy, or we'll be out here all afternoon. I think we all know you'd do the best job."

"She's right," Riley said. "I'm sorry I made it so hard, but I really was trying to help. The man could say anything. You did a good job, though. I thought asking for his address so you could go by his store was great."

"Yeah, if only he had been open!" Wendy retorted.

"What are you going to do if he says that?" Riley asked. "He could, you know."

"What would you say, Mr. Knows-Everything?"

"You can't be sidetracked by details. Ask him when he will be open. You might be able to sell him a grand opening ad."

"You should make this call," Wendy told him. "You obviously know more about selling than I do."

"I don't want to," he said, nudging the ground with the toe of his tennis shoe. "It's different selling things for school. If you can't sell all your stuff, your parents will buy it, or your grandparents. This is too important, and if I messed it up I would feel awful."

Wendy looked at Libby, even though she knew better. "Don't look at me. As soon as he answered the phone, I'd lose my voice."

"You sissies!" Wendy whirled around and stomped across the street. She hadn't even thought about what she would say to Myra, or whoever, about why she wanted to use the phone.

A bell tinkled on Myra's door as it swung shut behind her. Eight pairs of eyes, five of them under hair dryers, stared at her when she walked in. Of the other three women, one was having her platinum hair styled, one was waving a blow-dryer over it, and the third, with red tousled hair, was at the front counter with an appointment book open in front of her.

"Hi, Hon. We really can't take anybody else today," she said. "Tomorrow, though. We could give you a nice cut, take ten pounds off your face."

Wendy smiled her sweetest smile. "It's not my face that

needs to lose ten pounds," she said. The women all chuckled. "Do you think Mrs. Myra would let me use your phone?"

"Not Mrs. Myra, just Myra. And yes, I will. At least it won't ring while you're using it. But don't be too long."

"Thanks," said Wendy, picking up the phone Myra pushed toward her. She had hoped for a more private place, but this would have to do. At least it was a portable phone. She smiled at Myra, moved a bit closer to the door, and punched in the numbers. The phone rang almost seven times, and she was about to hang up when a voice answered:

"Rolling Things." It was a nice voice, but Wendy didn't understand the greeting.

"Ummm...what did you say?"

"Rolling Things," the voice repeated. "You know — things with wheels. Skates, skateboards, bicycles. Could I interest you in something that rolls?"

"Yes, maybe. Could you give me your address?"

"Sure. We're just off Main at 321 Webb."

"And you're open now?"

"Yes."

She thanked him and hung up. Webb was just around the corner. They could walk to Rolling Things in less than five minutes. It might be harder to talk to Paul Calhoun in person than on the phone, but at least she wouldn't have an audience when she did it.

"Through?" asked Myra as Wendy hung up. "You come back, now. Don't forget what I said about that cut. We could do something that would be cute with your dimples." She winked, and Wendy smiled and thanked her before she darted out the door.

"Come on!" she ordered her friends. "We're going to see Mr. Calhoun."

If Libby and Riley had questions, they knew better than to ask. They hurried to catch up. When Wendy stopped at the address, they looked at each other.

"We're going into this store, and we're going to ask for Mr. Calhoun, and then we're going to ask him to buy an ad in the *Bugle*."

"You didn't ask him on the phone?" said Libby.

"Studies show it's easier to sell something in person than over the phone," said Riley, before Wendy could answer. "Eye contact is important."

"Well, remember to contact his eyes when you try to sell the ad then," said Wendy.

Riley's face lost all color. "I can't. I wouldn't know...that is..."

"All right. I'll do the talking. But you are both coming in with me."

The edge in Wendy's voice told them not to argue. They followed her into the store. A young man came out to greet them.

"Could we speak to Mr. Calhoun?" Wendy asked. She felt a finger poking the small of her back and heard Libby's faint whisper: "Smile. Look pleasant."

Wendy gave the man a quick smile that she was sure looked fake and raised her eyebrows, wondering if she looked pleasant.

"I'm Paul Calhoun," said the man, smiling back. "I bet you three are here for in-line skates." He had curly black hair and dark eyes and was very handsome. Wendy felt fatter than ever and forgot what she wanted to say. As Paul Calhoun looked at her expectantly, she felt the finger poking her again. She just kept smiling.

She heard rustling behind her, and Riley stumbled forward,

as if pushed. He shot a look at Libby, then smiled nervously at Mr. Calhoun. "We like skating and all, but that's not why...um....we're here because...we got your number and..."

Hearing him fumble around brought Wendy's voice back. She looked directly into Paul Calhoun's dark eyes, smiled again, a real smile this time, and said, "We're here from the ad to sell you a *Bugle*."

As she heard her words, Wendy turned deep red. Mr. Calhoun was still smiling. "Try again," he suggested.

"I'm sorry," said Wendy, "but I haven't done this before. My friends and I are trying to help the *Bugle*. We want to sell you an ad." Miserable, she looked down at her feet and shook her head. "We'll be going now," she mumbled, motioning for the others to follow.

"Not so fast. Try it again," repeated Paul Calhoun. "Speaking to someone you don't know is just like skating for the first time. You need practice."

Here was a second chance. Wendy chewed on her lip as she thought about her words. She didn't want to mess this up. "We're from the *Bugle*," she said, "and we'd like to talk to you about advertising your business. Rolling Things is new, and you need to get the word out that you're here."

Mr. Calhoun rubbed his chin with his right hand. "Hmmm. Aren't you a little young to be selling ads?"

She thought about what he said for a moment. "I don't know how old you have to be," she said. "I know I read the ads in the paper. What age are most of your customers?"

Mr. Calhoun rubbed his chin harder, as if he was really thinking. "Your age, I guess, and a little older. And their parents, of course. They are the ones with the money."

"Who better than someone our age to tell you what kids like?"

"Kids read the paper?"

"I do," she responded. "We all do. We have to keep up with "Cheeky and Claude," for one thing."

"Cheeky and who?"

"Oh, you don't subscribe yet? You will have to start reading "Cheeky and Claude." It's the only comic strip in the paper, and it's only in the *Bugle*. Everyone's talking about it."

"You all skate?"

They looked at each other and Wendy wondered if Libby and Riley would contradict her if she lied. She decided they would. "No. We don't. But I would like to learn because I've read that it's good exercise and I need to lose weight. And we all ride bikes. You sell bikes and accessories, right?"

Paul Calhoun grinned. "That's good," he said. "You're very good at this!"

They stared at each other. Wendy knew he still hadn't decided to buy an ad. Wondering what else she could say, she glanced around his shop. The bright yellow walls and ceilings spiced the displays of the neon blue and hot pink-and-black skates and red skateboards. Hung from the ceiling were a few bicycles, all red. Most of the bikes were on the floor.

On the wall behind the front counter were framed certificates, one from a skateboarding club, another from the Carter County Nature Conservancy, another from Cyclists of America — wait a minute. Her eyes traveled back to the nature certificate, framed in a bright red square.

"You're a member of the county nature group? Did you see the story in the *Bugle* about Planet Friendly Plastics? I bet your group is happy about that."

"Well, I don't know about that, either. What's the story?" Wendy flashed a triumphant look at her friends. She told him the whole story of the new plastics plant and its business of selling items made from recycled plastics. "It's not popular with everyone, though," she added. "Some of the business owners here are afraid they'll have to pay their workers more to keep them."

"That sounds like a good thing for most people," said Paul Calhoun. "I like Moffatt Corner. We moved here because my wife grew up in Marlett, and she likes this area. But it needs more businesses so people can work in town instead of driving to Marlett or somewhere else."

"It needs a newspaper, too, which needs people like you to survive," said Wendy.

Paul Calhoun nodded. "You are right," he said. He walked to the checkout counter and pulled out a large notebook. They left a few minutes later with an order from Paul Calhoun for a two-column advertisement for a free skating lesson with a purchase of in-line skates. He gave Wendy a check for that and for a subscription and told Wendy she should come back next week to talk about more ads. Wendy felt as if she were flying through the clouds.

———— Eight ————

Tina to the Rescue

Wendy talked Libby and Riley into going back to the *Bugle* with her right away, even though Riley pointed out that the Rolling Things check probably would pay only for office supplies.

"It's not just the amount," argued Wendy, "it's the fact that he bought anything from us! They didn't think we could do it, and we did!"

Tina didn't say anything, but led them back to Luella's office. Luella was not impressed. "Not a very big ad," she said, and sniffed.

"He bought a subscription, too," said Wendy.

"He would've anyway," she said, flicking a hand in the air as if swatting a fly.

"But we did what you said to do. You act like it was no big deal, but if it was so easy, why didn't YOU do it?"

Luella tried to stare her down, but Wendy wouldn't budge. When the editor looked away, Wendy looked at her companions for help. This was fruitless. Riley was cracking his knuckles and

Libby was twisting her hair around her index finger. Wendy turned back to Luella. "I thought after we sold the ad, we'd work here."

"You thought wrong, and you all need to go on home!" said Luella. She retreated behind her desk and wouldn't look at any of them.

"What about that fashion show Saturday?" asked Tina. Everyone had forgotten she was still there until she spoke.

"What about it?" demanded Luella, scowling at her.

"We don't have anyone to cover it, since you're going to Planet Friendly Plastics' open house and I'm covering the Moffatt Corner Cat Show."

"Why can't you do both?"

Tina shrugged. "The cat show lasts all day, with winners announced hourly."

"We'll just have to skip the fashion show, then," said Luella. "We can't be everywhere!"

"A-hem," Tina said, then jerked her head toward Wendy and her friends.

"Is your problem with your throat or just your head in general?" Luella snapped.

Tina stared at her silently, unblinking, face expressionless.

"No," the editor said.

"Why not? Look what they did with their first assignment."

"He was a cream puff. What do they know about fashion?"

Wendy felt sharply aware of her shapeless gray sweats. She glanced at Riley in his jeans and Libby in her baby clothes. Them covering a fashion show? Luella was right.

"Well, I'll go to the fashion show and skip the cats," said Tina.

"Everybody wants to read about the cats!" yelled Luella, her face red.

Tina shrugged. "You will recall that we didn't cover the fashion show last year, and everyone called the next day. Several people canceled their subscriptions. But it's your decision." She looked at Wendy and raised her eyebrows. Wendy took the cue.

"We know lots about fashion," she fibbed. "Libby and I can ask questions. Riley can take pictures. What time does the show start?" A finger punched the small of her back. She couldn't tell which of her cowardly friends it was and didn't care.

"What do you know about covering a story?" thundered Luella. "That's a job for a reporter!"

"And selling an ad was a job for a salesperson, but we did that! What if we sell more ads between now and Saturday? Then will you let us cover the fashion show?" The finger poked her harder this time, but she was busy facing down Luella again. They stared at each other for at least half a minute before Luella finally averted her eyes. Wendy was elated. She had won her second stare-down.

"All right," growled Luella. "Sell five more ads. If you cover that story, I want a fresh angle on it. And if you bungle it, I never want to see you again in this office. And you!" She pointed to Tina. "You should mind your own business!"

"That's what I'm doing," Tina said sweetly. She hustled them out of the office and up to her desk. "I've got three people here who I'm pretty sure will buy ads, but you guys are going to have to dig up at least two more on your own. Think you can do that?"

Wendy nodded hurriedly, taking Tina's list, and hoping she could get the other two out before they said anything. She barely made it.

"What have you gotten us into now?" cried Libby, once they

were outside. "Didn't you feel me poking you?"

"Yeah, how am I supposed to take pictures when I don't even have a camera?" Riley demanded.

"You can borrow your father's camera. You have before."

"Wenn-n-dy," breathed Libby, "do you have any idea how hard it is to write about a fashion show? You and Riley don't know a thing about clothes."

"Oh, and I suppose you do? Besides, Riley just takes pictures. He doesn't need to know anything."

"With what?" yelled Riley. "I don't own a camera! And when are we going to sell all these ads?"

Fury hit Wendy like a hot gust, its tongue lapping her face and turning it red. She stopped walking, forcing the other two, who had been behind her, to do the same, and stared them down without blinking. Even as wind whipped her hair into her eyes, she didn't stop.

"If I have to sell the ads by myself, then that's what I will do," she said, her voice calm and eyes blazing. "If I have to cover the show by myself, I will do that, too. I will do whatever it takes. You two can stay home and watch cartoons for all I care."

She stomped away, headed for home, or somewhere — she didn't really know. She told herself she didn't care if they followed, either. That wasn't true, but if she admitted even to herself that she did care, she would turn around and look, and that she could not do. Suddenly, someone grabbed her arm.

"Wait up!" Riley yelled.

Wendy turned around. He and Libby reached her, out of breath. "Don't be so impatient with us," he said. "We need a chance to get used to this idea. You've obviously been thinking about it a lot longer than we have…I can probably borrow my father's camera. If not, I'll find one somewhere. I'll work it out.

But what about the ads?"

Libby caught up. "I'll help, too. Sorry," she added, glancing at Wendy's red face before looking down at her feet.

They walked silently, three abreast, for half a block before anyone spoke again. It was Libby. "I have an idea," she said softly. "Each of us can take a name on that list and sell it. Then we only have two more."

"And I have an idea about that," said Wendy. "Myra was really nice to let me use her phone, and I've never seen her ads in the *Bugle*. I'm going to ask her. And maybe another person will occur to us between now and Saturday."

They walked without speaking for another block. Finally, Wendy broke the silence. "What do you think she meant by a fresh angle?"

Libby shook her head.

"I think she meant we should look for things you wouldn't normally write about in a fashion story," said Riley.

"Then fresh should be easy, since we've never written one," said Wendy. "I've never even been to a fashion show. Have either of you?"

Riley shook his head.

"I have," Libby said in her quiet voice. Riley and Wendy stopped walking and stared at her. Wendy thought she knew everything about her friend, but she didn't know about this.

"It's the Moffatt Corner Easter show, and my mom makes me go with her every year," said Libby, her face pink. "They show lots of spring clothes and hats. Most of the clothes are from Marlett, and so people come from there, and everyone dresses up. My mom can't go this year, thank goodness. But she will be overjoyed that I'm going."

Wendy stared at her. "You go every year? You're an expert, then!"

"Not quite. Remember, my mom goes, too, and she's the one who picks out my clothes."

"Still, you know more than us." Wendy paused, an idea forming. "Libby, don't women wear hats to that show? What are they like?"

"Big ones, small ones," said Libby, shrugging. "Straw and cloth, and some have flowers or fruit. Once in awhile, you see a really funny one. One last year looked like a cooking pot without the handle."

"What if we wrote about the hats women wear to the show? You know, hat fashion in Moffatt Corner."

"That's a good idea," said Libby, the color in her face back to normal.

"And you could also write about the regular clothes that are being modeled, right? I mean, since you've been there before, you know what to write about — what's in, what's out."

"I guess I could," said Libby. "But I don't know much," she said, doubt creeping into her voice.

"You probably know more than most of the people who'll be there. And Riley can get pictures. Let's talk about the questions we'll need to ask."

"How much did that cost?" offered Riley.

"You don't ask that," Libby said. You find out, but you never ask. Not like that."

"Yeah, Riley, even I know that," added Wendy.

"I thought that was important."

"It is, but you're supposed to find out some other way, or at least ask later," Wendy said.

He didn't say any more, just listened to the two girls talk about fabric and hem length and walking shorts and whether trousers were going to be full-legged or slim. Wendy, who had a small notebook in her pocket, scribbled their ideas as fast as she could write. They agreed to compare ad sales and go over last-minute plans for the fashion show in two days.

When the time came for them to part ways and head home, Wendy watched until the other two were out of sight and headed back to Myra's House of Beauty. She wanted to try to sell at least one more ad today.

But Myra shook her head at Wendy's request. "Hon, I have all the business I need. I'm booked up every day of the week from eight to six. An ad in the Bugle would just mean more operators, which I don't have room for, or more hours, which I don't want."

Wendy looked at her thoughtfully. "Do you do something here that not enough people know about? Something that you wish more people would do while they're under dryers or something?"

Myra's eyes brightened. "Why, yes we do – manicures. One of my girls is excellent at it, but nobody ever thinks about it. She needs more customers, too."

"What if you took out a small ad for manicures and maybe put a coupon in it, just to get people to try it? Then you could tape the ad to the counter – it would be like an extra ad, a reminder."

Myra asked if she'd get a price break for putting the ad in more than once, and after a quick call back to Tina to determine size and prize, she'd sold Myra's House of Beauty an ad for a whole month of *Bugles*. Then Myra pointed her to a sandwich shop that had just opened and needed business, and Wendy headed there next. The owner wasn't there, but she got his name and number. On her way out, she noticed huge slices of pie displayed in a glass case. The chocolate meringue caught her eye first. Then she saw coconut cream and apple.

"Are those made here?" she asked the cashier, who nodded. Once out on the sidewalk, she wrote "pies" by the owner's name. Then she hurried home, worried that her mother would be calling Libby's house to find her.

But her mother was deep into a project of her own, something she called a Deep Dish Cheese Pie. Wendy retreated to her room, relieved that Wanda hadn't noticed how late she'd gotten home.

—— Nine ——

A Puff of Wind, a Dog, a Hat

Before school Friday, they gave their reports. Wendy had convinced the sandwich shop owner that his pies were a treasure he should advertise. Everyone knew by the shop's name, Wheat or White?, that he sold sandwiches. But the homemade pies set him apart, she said. Then when she dropped Myra's name, he told her to "sign him up" for the same deal.

Wendy worried a bit that she hadn't sold another ad, but she needn't have. Libby and Riley had sold three ads between them. "It wasn't as hard as I thought it would be," said Riley. "I called the computer store where my dad shops and told them that they should tell people when they got in new software because they are the only computer store in town. And that guy told me about a card and stationery shop next door, so I called them, too. It was pretty easy."

One of the names Tina had given them turned out to be Libby's ballet teacher, who wanted to advertise her dance school. "I told her I hadn't been there because I'd been sick, and she felt sorry for me. Maybe that's why she bought an ad," said Libby.

"Oh, and my dad said I could borrow his camera," reported Riley. "I told him it was for a project."

"And I've been reading about the new spring clothes," said Libby. "They're supposed to be 'swingy and springy.' I guess that means loose-fitting, light fabrics." The other two nodded, impressed that Libby had figured that out. They agreed that Wendy would take all the ad information to Tina after school, and that they would meet the next morning at the school gym, at least thirty minutes before the show started.

Tina was stunned with their progress. "I'm going to call each of them and see if they want to set up an account," she said. "And Myra's House of Beauty and the sandwich shop both want to advertise for a month? We may make you and Libby and Riley full-time salespeople!"

"Does this mean we get to cover the fashion show?"

Tina nodded. "You were going to anyway, weren't you?" she asked, smiling slightly. "Don't answer that. Just go and cover it. You need to come back right after it's over and write your story and give us the film so we can get it in the next edition."

Wendy began to get butterflies in her stomach before she ever went to bed. When dawn finally arrived Saturday morning, her legs felt as if there were blocks of iron strapped to them. Thirty minutes before she was supposed to meet Libby and Riley, she stared into her closet, her worn blue bathrobe knotted tight around her waist. What did she have to wear to a fashion show?

She had her hands on the gray sweats folded neatly on a shelf when she spied the black trousers hanging far back in her closet. She had begged her mother to buy them last Christmas after reading a *Bugle* story about how dark colors were thinning.

She had never worn the pants, though, because they had

been too tight from the very first. She had adopted the gray sweats as a uniform right after Christmas and had noticed that people didn't look at her when she wore gray. That's when she decided to spend her allowance money to buy five gray sweatshirts and five pairs of gray sweatpants so she would have a set for almost every day of the week.

But Libby had told her to wear something else today. "I promise that people will stare at you if you come to a fashion show in sweats, gray or not," she'd said. "Take it from an expert at getting stared at. Just wear something conservative, then no one will even remember five minutes later what you had on."

Wendy put the black pants on her bed and searched for her black turtleneck, which she had worn only a couple of times. It should look all right with the pants, and it was comfortable and lightweight enough for spring.

She pulled on the pants slowly, holding her breath, and was elated when they slid on and buttoned easily. Her mother refused to buy a scale so she didn't know that she had lost weight. You couldn't tell much one way or the other with sweats, and Wendy never looked in the mirror. But she had walked or ridden her bike almost everywhere for a month, and had managed to eat less, despite her mother's cooking. That had been the hardest. Her mother gave her the third degree if she left anything uneaten, so she'd had to think of creative ways to hide what she didn't eat and throw it away later.

She waited until she was completely dressed to look at herself in the full-length mirror in her mother's closet. She only peeked, expecting to see a fat girl dressed like a cat burglar. Instead, her eyes saw a face with pink cheeks and bright brown eyes.

"Huh," she said. "Black looks good on me. Maybe people

will just focus on the face and forget the fat parts." She let her eyes go downward, slowly toward her waist and her thighs. She held her breath at what she saw, then closed her eyes for a moment and opened them again. Was it really her own reflection? Yes, it was. And it looked pretty good. She wasn't as fat as she thought.

A slamming door made her jump. She checked her watch and realized she was going to be late. She dashed back to her room, slipped her feet into black loafers and hurriedly combed her hair.

But as soon as she smelled the waffles and sausage, Wendy knew getting out of the house would be tricky. There was no time for breakfast, and she hadn't told her mother anything about the *Bugle* or the fashion show.

"Mom!" she called, edging toward the front door, "I can't eat breakfast this morning. I'm going to help Libby study for a test. See you later!" She squeezed her eyes shut, put her hand on the doorknob and turned it.

Before she could open the door even a crack, Wanda was in the hallway holding a spatula. Every hair was in place and she was dressed all in red. She would look just fine at a fashion show. Wendy thought briefly about asking her to go along. They could use the help.

"Why do you need to see Libby this early? And why are you so dressed up?"

"She's real nervous about the test. I'll be back this afternoon," she said, opening the door.

"Wait a minute!" said her mother. She walked up right behind Wendy and tapped her on the shoulder with the spatula. Wendy braced for the questions she knew were coming as her mother looked her up and down.

"Are you losing weight? You should not be skipping breakfast! It's the most important meal of the day."

Wendy considered her options. She could throw a tantrum, which would not work, or she could be honest. She smiled broadly at her mother. "I hope I am losing weight, but how would I know? We don't have a scale. How about if I eat something at Libby's?" Not totally honest, but not a total lie, either.

Her mother's eyes searched her face, and Wendy flushed. She felt guilty. Would her mother know?

"Oh, I guess it's all right, this once," said Wanda with a sigh. "I'd take you over there, but I can't just turn off the food. It would all ruin. What time will you be home this afternoon?"

"Two?" Wendy asked, relieved that she could take her bike. Then she fled, pedaling furiously to the gym. She thought the exercise would clear her mind, but it worked the other way; the harder she pedaled, the guiltier she felt about her lie.

Both Libby's and Riley's bikes were already locked in the parking lot rack. She left hers beside them and hurried inside, clutching her notebook. She immediately spotted them in the back. They looked like they expected to be kicked out at any moment.

"Remind me again why we're doing this," whispered Libby. She was in ruffles from her neck to the tip of her hem. She carried a ruffled drawstring purse made of the same fabric as her dress.

"I see your mother's been sewing again," said Wendy.

"Quit trying to change the subject. In case you haven't noticed, we are very much out of place here. I think we should just go and forget all about this."

Wendy looked from Libby to Riley, who wore nice jeans, a dark blue denim shirt and a bright red tie. Hanging from a leather strap around his neck was his father's camera, and the lenses of his glasses were clean for once. He looked handsome.

She glanced around the gym at the crowd. It was made up mostly of women. Except for a small child here and there, they were the only ones younger than thirty. They wore dresses in all colors, styles and sizes. Some looked good and some did not. One woman in an expensive suit and high heels wore an orange cloth hat that looked like a clay flower pot, and it actually had a flower on the top of it. But because of the way the hat was shaped, the flower appeared to be growing out of the wrong end of the pot. A bit of the woman's hair peeked out the bottom. Something about her looked familiar. Wendy stared at her for a moment before the woman noticed her staring. Wendy quickly looked away.

"I think you two look just fine," said Wendy. "What about me? How do I look?"

"Nice," said Riley. "New clothes?"

"Fine, I guess," Libby responded in a monotone as she looked around the room. "Wendy, I don't have a clue about what to write."

"Of course you don't. The show hasn't started yet." She saw some empty chairs near the front, took Libby by the arm and motioned Riley to follow. "Look," she said, bringing her chair around so she faced Libby, "You read fashion magazines all the time, right?"

Libby nodded haltingly.

"You already know fashion, then. And you're always looking at what people are wearing and telling me what you think. Didn't you tell me not to wear sweats today? How do I look?" Wendy repeated, leaning back in her chair, arms spread wide.

Libby couldn't suppress her grin. "Like a burglar. Or a country singer."

"Thank you. And thinner too, right?"

Libby's eyes started at the turtleneck and went down to the

hem on Wendy's black, straight-legged trousers, then came back to Wendy's eyes.

"Yes. You look very classic. If only you had a gold chain around your neck — "

"A gold chain!" said Wendy, smacking herself in the forehead. "Why didn't I think of that? I look at me and see a pig in training. You look at me and see the possibilities. See, Libby, that's what I mean."

"You're not making fun of me, are you?" Libby's eyes flicked quickly from Wendy's face to Riley's, then back to Wendy's.

"Nope. I mean it. You know what to do. Just use your instincts. I wish I had any." She leaned back and sighed, looking around the room. That's when she saw Roomer, lying at the gym's back door on his belly, head on his paws, sleek chocolate coat gleaming in a puddle of sun. His eyes were black slits, but Wendy knew from experience he wasn't really sleeping.

"Who let him in?" she asked.

Riley shrugged. "Guess he figures he has a right to be here. After all, it is his home."

Part Lab and part unknown, Roomer had been the middle school dog the past two years. He showed up one day and stayed, thanks to a kindly school maintenance crew and teachers who fed him regularly, made sure his shots were up-to-date, and gave him a warm, dry place to sleep when the weather was bad. He was a friendly, playful dog with a shiny coat, his only physical flaw a three-inch scar on the top of his head near his left ear. He'd arrived at the school with it, and one of the teachers who saw to his medical needs speculated it was the result of a sore that had been left untreated in his earlier life.

Spoiled from all the attention, Roomer would have been fat from treats alone except for recess. Someone had taught him to fetch Frisbees. Most of the time he brought them back.

Just then a woman dressed in a lacy pink dress stepped to the microphone and asked everyone to be seated.

"You ready?" Wendy whispered to the other two. Libby didn't answer, but Riley nodded.

The models' runway consisted of homemade ramps coming from two doors, one on either side of the gym. The ramps inclined downward gently and formed a "v." They connected in the center of the gym. From there, one runway path continued to a single platform. The models were supposed to come out of the doors at the same time, each walking down her ramp, meet at the point of the "v," continue walking down the single runway arm-in-arm, turn at the platform and return to the side opposite the one they'd entered.

The runway idea might have worked if the models had been able to keep up with the fast-paced music. But it was clear they were unfamiliar with both the beat and the runway. Some hesitated at the "crossroads" as if wondering which way to go, making those coming behind them bump into them. After the third collision, Libby looked at Wendy and rolled her eyes.

"This is terrible," she muttered. "Why can't they slow them down a little?"

"I guess the music just makes everyone hurry," Wendy whispered. "You're going to have to write about this."

"You think?"

"Has it ever happened before when you were here?"

Libby shook her head.

"Then you have to say what happened."

"The clothes are nice," said Libby.

Wendy nodded, glad she didn't have to write about them. She wouldn't know what to say. She turned to watch Riley get pictures. He didn't know which outfits to take pictures of, and was sitting on the floor at the end of the runway, shooting everything.

Suddenly, a spring gust blew through the open side doors. While some women were able to clamp their hands over their heads and save their hats, the flower pot woman was not so lucky. The flower was caught by the breeze. Her hat bounced across the gym floor.

"My hat!" she cried, getting up to chase it.

Several men and women rose to help her, running after the upside-down flower pot almost in step with the runway music. The models stopped to watch, as did the commentator.

Wendy stood up and craned her neck. She saw the hat skittering straight toward her. She didn't even notice that Riley was taking picture after picture.

Wendy grabbed for it and almost had it, but the wind changed course and the hat flew in another direction. It went from air to floor, where it looked like a big orange pot rolling on its side. Wendy raced for it.

"I think I have it," she yelled, just before Roomer lunged in front of her, grabbed the hat and sped away.

The hat's owner screamed, "That hat cost a fortune! You must get it back!"

Wendy, horrified, was unable to move. She suddenly knew who the woman was. It had to be Mrs. Horton! Burnam looked just like her! She hardly ever appeared in public, but apparently she liked fashion shows.

"Roomer!" Wendy yelled.

"Is that your dog?" a man shouted at her. "Bring him back here at once!"

But it was too late. Roomer had his prize, and he wasn't about to give it up. He scrambled out the gym door, back feet slipping crazily on the glossy floor, but not slowing enough for anyone to nab him. He disappeared with the hat locked firmly in his jaws.

"Why'd you bring a mutt to a fashion show anyway?" the man yelled at Wendy.

"My hat! My beautiful spring hat!" wailed Mrs. Horton.

All the time, Riley was taking pictures and the music was blasting cheerfully.

"Did you get a picture of the dog with the hat?" Wendy asked Riley.

"At least a dozen."

"Good. It'll go with the extra story we're going to write," she said, hurrying off to interview Mrs. Horton.

Ten

Busted!

The following Wednesday Wendy awoke to silence and realized something wasn't right. She thought she'd set the alarm to get up early so she could grab the *Bugle* first. She still hadn't told her parents she was working for the paper, and Luella had put their fashion show coverage on page one. She had planned to break the news to her parents early in the morning.

But it wasn't early. It was seven, and her alarm had not gone off. Both her parents would already be up. She dressed hurriedly and tiptoed to the kitchen, hoping her father had taken the paper to work with him. He did that sometimes, and he would never read a fashion story. And if he took the paper with him, her mother wouldn't think to ask for it.

The kitchen looked normal. Her mother was at the sink, squeezing oranges. "Hello, Wendy," she said, without turning around.

"Morning," Wendy mumbled as she sank into a chair. "How do you do that?"

"What?"

"Know who it is without even looking."

"Process of elimination," said Wanda. "By the way, you never told me — how did the test go?"

"What test?" Wendy said, yawning. She gulped and her heart skipped. The *Bugle* was on the kitchen counter, right next to her mother's left elbow. She wanted badly to grab it, but she didn't dare.

"The test you helped Libby study for Saturday morning." Her mother turned around and looked right into Wendy's eyes.

"Oh, that test," stalled Wendy as she tried to get her brain to work. She made invisible slashes with the nail of her right index finger on the crisp white tablecloth. Apparently, the cat was out of the bag and she'd have to explain herself. Not that there was anything wrong with what she and her friends were doing, but her mother would find plenty about it not to like. She could start with the lie she'd told Saturday morning. It was clear that whatever happened, she couldn't lie again. She wasn't any good at it and it made her feel terrible.

"I never went to Libby's," Wendy said, her voice faint. "I was with Libby, though. She and Riley and I are working for the *Bugle*. We covered the Easter fashion show Saturday."

Her mother turned away and began again squeezing the orange half in the pointed glass juicer. Wendy wondered how there could be any juice left. She timed the silence, watching the second hand on the kitchen clock. It lasted almost a minute. She eyed the *Bugle* again.

"So you told me a lie. When do you go to the *Bugle*, and how long have you been working there? And what other lies have you told me?"

Wanda got right to the point. She would make a good reporter.

"I haven't told you any other lies." Wendy's voice was a monotone. "We work at the *Bugle* after school. We haven't done much – the fashion show was our first assignment. That and selling some ads. It took awhile for us to convince Ms. Cathcart to let us work."

"Who?"

"Luella Cathcart, the editor. First she made us sell ads, then she let us cover the fashion show."

"How much is she paying you?"

"We're working for free. She can't afford to pay us." Wendy slashed the tablecloth with her fingernail again. Her desire to go to the counter and get the *Bugle* was almost overwhelming.

"I see. What a great deal," said Wanda. Her tone said, "How stupid do I look?"

"It is a great deal if we help keep the paper operating!" cried Wendy. "I don't mind working for free if it means I'm doing something important!"

Her mother soaped her hands and rubbed them together. She rinsed them for a long time, then wiped them dry. "So you see this as important volunteer work? This was your idea, Wendy, wasn't it? What do Libby and Riley's parents say about it?"

Wendy breathed deeply. "I'm not sure they know." Her mother didn't say anything, just nodded her head ever so slightly, as if she'd known what her daughter was going to say. "Well," added Wendy, "I guess they do now." Changing the subject was probably stupid, but Wendy decided to give it a shot.

"So I guess you read my story, huh?"

Her mother nodded. "Your father pointed it out to me this morning."

"Dad read it?" she asked, stunned.

"It was the first thing he noticed. He thought it was funny, and told me I should read it. I didn't know I was going to be reading a story by my own daughter."

"So," said Wendy, trying to sound lighthearted, " what did you think? Is the story all right?"

Her mother was still wiping her hands on a towel, even though they weren't wet. "I am not worried about how good the story is, Wendy. I just don't know what to think. You lied to me. You led your friends to lie to their parents. You're running all over town, talking to people I don't know. You've written a story about poor Mrs. Horton, whose hat was taken by a dog. It's hard enough to live in a small town without your daughter making fun of people in the paper. Whether or not your writing is good is not at the top of my list."

"I didn't make fun of anyone!" cried Wendy. "Is that what you think? Is that what Dad thought? I just told what happened. It was a silly hat, but I didn't make fun of her for wearing it or anything!"

Her mother poured a glass of juice and set it down, hard, in front of Wendy. Then she turned away to gaze out of the window. "I knew you were the ringleader," she said, as if Wendy hadn't spoken. "You always have been. I suppose with Miranda it was necessary." Wanda stopped abruptly.

Her mother had always been a little angry at Wendy that Miranda was the disabled one, maybe even blamed her a bit. Miranda was the "good" daughter, the sweet one, the one who never got into trouble and never caused anyone to worry. Wendy knew this even though the words had never been said.

"I'm sorry for lying, Mom," she said, offering the only thing she could. "I should have told you what we were doing, but I didn't think you'd let me do any of this if you knew. I won't lie to you again. I promise. And I haven't lied to you before."

Her mother didn't answer. Wendy drained the juice glass and glanced around the kitchen. Her mother hadn't fixed anything, so she got a bowl of Cheerios and tried to eat quickly. But in the silence of the kitchen, her chewing sounded like footfalls on a gravel path. Self-conscious at the noise, she dumped half the bowl of cereal into the garbage disposal.

Her mother hadn't packed her a lunch. "Guess I'll ride my bike to school," said Wendy. It was half-question and half-statement. Wanda nodded silently and kept gazing out the window. On impulse, Wendy walked over, put her arms around her mother's waist and leaned her head against Wanda's back. Wendy couldn't be certain, but she thought she felt her mother hold her breath. Wendy knew Wanda must be thinking of an appropriate punishment.

She eyed the *Bugle* one last time and thought again about grabbing it, then decided that would not be wise. "Bye," she said. She felt terrible for making her mother so sad, but she was relieved to get away. Then she felt terrible for feeling relieved, and wondered what her punishment would be.

Libby and Riley waited for her outside school. Libby had a long face, but Riley looked cheerful. "So," said Wendy, locking up her bike, "I see both of you survived."

"We should have thought more about doing something so public!" cried Libby. "The *Bugle* story with the line at the bottom saying I contributed was like the first thing my mother saw. She freaked!"

"What did she say?" asked Wendy, afraid to admit she hadn't seen the story.

"She demanded to know why I hadn't told her what I was doing. And she still doesn't know I've been skipping ballet. I am dead when she finds out!"

"So are you grounded?"

"No." Libby shook her head. "That would be a relief. At least I'd know what she's thinking. But I don't think she knows herself what she is going to do."

Wendy looked at Riley. "I didn't get in trouble," he said, shrugging. "I guess the photo credits are too small. No one even noticed. But they probably wouldn't care anyway. What about your parents?" he asked Wendy.

"Dad wasn't there. But Mom – she was strange. She asked me why I lied, too. But she was sad and quiet. It was really weird. She didn't even make breakfast. I wish she had freaked out. It would have been easier to deal with that."

"So what do we do today?" Riley asked Wendy. Libby looked at her, too.

"You mean, do we go back to the *Bugle*?"

Riley nodded.

She looked from him to Libby. "Well, I'm going. I hope you guys come, too, because the *Bugle* needs help, and I can't do it alone."

"I'm in," said Riley.

"Guess so," sighed Libby. "Until my mom figures out what to do to me, anyway. But you'd better figure out a way to get more help because I might not be able to do this much longer."

Wendy nodded. "I promise I will get more help. I just need time."

As it turned out, there was no time. As soon as she finished calling the roll, Mrs. Martino asked who had read the *Bugle* that morning. For once, Wendy did not raise her hand, but no one noticed. Everyone else's hands shot into the air except for five or six at the back of the room.

"So you all know that we have some *Bugle* reporters and photographers in our midst!" said Mrs. Martino, smiling widely.

Wendy felt her face turn red; sweat trickled down her back,

between her shoulder blades. She knew her fringe of bangs would soon be plastered down, and she was conscious of a growing dampness under her arms. She looked at Libby, who was looking down at her desk, her arms folded across her chest. "Wendy?" said Mrs. Martino. "Would you like to tell the class about your adventures with the *Bugle*?"

Dozens of curious eyes focused on her. She wanted to charge out of the room and never return. She wished suddenly that Wanda had home-schooled her. She cleared her throat. "Yes," she heard her voice say and was surprised that it sounded normal. "We originally went to the *Bugle* office to volunteer to do anything just to help keep it going. But the editor didn't want us at first. Well, I'm still not sure she does even now." She heard some giggles and blushed again.

"Volunteer!" spat Burnam. "Correct me if I'm wrong, but that means no pay, right?"

Wendy started to ignore him, then remembered how he grew quiet when Mrs. Martino talked to him directly.

"Yes, Burnam," she said. "I don't want the *Bugle* to close. That's why I volunteered to help. I convinced Libby Weaver and Riley Davis to go with me and see what we could do." Her eyes rested on his and didn't move, and he looked away. "Maybe you saw our story and pictures in today's paper," she said to the class at large. "It was our first assignment. We covered the Easter fashion show, and we had fun. We didn't know how to write the story, but the editor and her assistant helped us."

"And you made fun of a woman losing her hat!" said Burnam, then immediately turned red. He had said too much. He hadn't raised his hand when Mrs. Martino asked who had read the *Bugle*, but he obviously knew what the story was about and that his mother was featured in it.

"Not that I saw the story," he added. "I heard about it. Fashion's not my thing. And even if it was, I wouldn't read what you wrote about clothes, and I sure wouldn't read anything in the *Bugle*. I knew it was a rag, but volunteers? Sheesh!"

His pals burst into laughter. Giggles and titters rippled throughout the room. Wendy looked at Mrs. Martino for help. The teacher smiled at her, but didn't say anything. Both Libby and Riley were red-faced and staring down at their desks. At a loss for words, Wendy tried to think what to say next. But she didn't have to say anything.

"You've got it all wrong, Burnam," piped up a voice from the front of the room, silencing the snickers. "Wendy and Libby and Riley didn't just report about fashion. The real story was about Roomer stealing a hat at the show. I've never seen anything like it before in the *Bugle*. It was funny! And everyone in town is talking about it. And no one made fun of that woman. It was all told in a very factual way!"

Wendy grinned at the speaker, a pretty girl with long, dark hair and dancing blue-black eyes. Her name was Carmen Degarcia. Carmen may have been the only girl in school who could say what she had just said to Burnam and still have anyone to talk to. She didn't run around with any group, and the unspoken rule at Riddle Middle School seemed to be the less you needed friends, the more friends you had.

"What happened to the hat after Roomer got it?" asked someone else, a student who hadn't seen the story.

Carmen looked at Wendy, who kept quiet. "Their story said neither Roomer nor the hat came back. Who knows? It may turn up at school."

"What did the hat look like?" someone else asked.

Carmen looked again at Wendy, but it was Libby who answered this time. "It looked like an upside-down flower pot with the flower growing out of the bottom – or out of the top of the lady's head. The lady who was wearing it, I mean."

She hadn't meant it to be funny, but the class erupted in laughter.

"Roomer probably buried it because it was ugly!" someone called out, and everyone laughed again. Everyone except Burnam, who glared at everyone who spoke.

When the laughter faded, Wendy spoke quickly. "Does anyone want to volunteer? You may not have much time to work, but even if you had only an hour a week, you could do something at the *Bugle*."

"Why should we work without pay?" Burnam demanded, his face red.

"Yeah!" seconded one of his friends.

"Because the *Bugle* can't pay. The editor has laid off just about everybody. We're just trying to help keep it going until the editor figures out what to do." She thought for just a moment before adding, "One of the biggest advertisers pulled his ads out and asked other people to do the same thing. Advertising is a newspaper's major source of income. If the *Bugle* gets some more advertisers, maybe it can stay open."

"I don't know why we should care if the *Bugle* stays open," Burnam said with a shrug. "What's it done for us?"

"Just last month the newspaper helped sponsor the band's pancake supper, which helped pay for the band's trip to Washington, D.C.," said Mrs. Martino. "Last year, it helped with the cleanup of the soccer field, and then paid for part of the bleachers."

"But there aren't many stories in the paper that interest us," said a boy in the back.

"You are the cure for that," said Mrs. Martino. "You want stories in the paper for you, about you? Wendy is offering you the chance to find them and write them. Isn't that right?" She looked at Wendy, who nodded.

"I think we should write about Roomer," said Carmen. "Has anyone seen him since the fashion show? And where does he really live when we go home at night?"

Heads were nodding.

"We could write about the food in the cafeteria," said someone else. "We had beef stew three days in a row last week. Leftover leftovers."

Mrs. Martino turned to Wendy. "Would you like to send around a signup sheet for volunteers?"

Wendy quickly started a sheet of paper at the front. "If you can volunteer, put your phone number and what day you can work beside your name," she said. As she watched the sheet of paper go from hand to hand, stopping at some desks, Mrs. Martino squeezed her arm.

"You did very well," she whispered. "But don't be surprised if you get more names than actual volunteers."

"What do you mean?" asked Wendy.

"You'll see."

When the paper returned to her, it was filled with names and phone numbers. She was sure that the *Bugle*'s future was guaranteed.

—— Eleven ——

The Readers Speak

Where have you been?" Luella demanded as Wendy, Riley and Libby walked into the *Bugle* offices that afternoon. "The phone has been ringing all day!" Standing at Tina's desk, she leaned her short, square body toward them, arms crossed, her eyes boring into them, foot tapping on the floor. Her short white hair was standing straight up in places.

"School," Wendy said, frowning. "Remember? We go to school."

"You have a job here. Remember?" Luella retorted.

Wendy shook her book bag off her shoulders and onto a nearby table. "We're working for free, but that doesn't mean we're your slaves. We still have to go to school."

Luella glared. "Just like all reporters, you have a smart mouth. I have assignments for you," she said, just as the phone rang. "That's probably for you," she pointed to the phone as if she expected Wendy to answer.

Tina, her mouth making a disapproving frown, shook her head at Luella and picked it up. "*Bugle* office, Tina Majors. Yes," she said, after listening a moment. "Uh-huh. Why yes, that's right. Oh? Really? How do you spell that? And the phone number?" She cradled the phone between her shoulder and ear and pawed around on her desk with both hands for her notebook and pen. Then she scribbled hurriedly. "OK, I'll tell them. Yes. Glad you liked it. Yes, I'm sure you will."

"Another one?" demanded Luella as Tina hung up.

"Someone offered our new reporters a story idea. That was one of the good ones," Tina added. She counted the slash marks on her notepad. "Twenty-two, so far."

"And how many on the other list?"

Tina counted silently. "Fourteen."

The editor shook her head. "Not good. Not good at all." She looked at the floor, rubbing her wrinkled forehead.

Tina caught Wendy's eye and winked, and Wendy managed a confused smile. She had no idea what was going on. She glanced at Libby and Riley, who looked as if they were trying to decide whether to make a run for it. The phone rang again.

"I'll get this one," announced Luella, reaching across Tina to pick up the phone. "Hello, *Bugle* office!" she barked. "Yes, yes, Wendy Wright is my reporter. Yes, so is the other one. Her name is Libby Weaver. Yes, he's the photographer." She stopped talking and listened, scowling. Slowly the scowl disappeared. "Yes, hiring them was my idea. Yes, thank you. Of course I intend to keep them. Thank you again. Goodbye."

She banged down the phone. "Twenty-three," she said to Tina, then turned to Wendy. "And don't think that call gets you off the hook. You should have been here all day so you could have talked to the people who are mad."

"What are they mad about?" asked Wendy.

Glaring, Luella grabbed that day's edition of the paper and read the first paragraph of Wendy's story about the fashion show:

"Roomer the dog took a fancy to a flower-pot hat worn to the Easter fashion show Saturday, and neither the dog nor the head covering has been seen since."

The editor looked up from the sentence and glared at Wendy again.

"What's wrong with that?" Wendy asked. "You even helped me write it."

Luella kept glaring. Wendy glared back. After a few seconds, Luella plopped into a chair and held her head in her hands.

"There's nothing wrong with it! That's what makes me so mad! It's a really good story and people are complaining about it."

"Doesn't that happen with some stories?" asked Wendy. "Everyone's not going to like it, even if there's nothing wrong with it."

"Well, you should have insisted that Mrs. Horton talk to you! If she had said something, anything, it would have been better than saying she turned around and walked away!"

"But that's what she did. I tried to talk to her, but she just waved me away. But the story isn't about her. It's about what the dog did."

"Yeah," chimed in Libby, who had edged into the office. "Why does it matter whose hat it was?"

"You!" said Luella, pointing at Libby. "I can't believe you called the show 'a giant traffic jam of colliding bodies!' "

Libby looked at Tina, who suddenly got very busy straightening papers on her desk. "I had help writing, too," Libby said. "And anyway, that's what happened. The models bumped into each other the whole time. They could have practiced before-hand."

"Did someone call complaining about how we treated Mrs. Horton?" Wendy asked, trying to get Libby off the hook.

"She called herself, and she was yelling and crying. And she said she was going to sue us for slander!"

"Can she do that?" Wendy asked.

Luella didn't answer because the phone rang again. Tina grabbed it. "Hello, Bu—" she began, then fell silent, listening. After a moment, she put the receiver down. "Fifteen," she said to Luella, marking another slash on the notepad.

"Fifteen mad calls," Luella said, shaking her head. "Ten subscriptions canceled."

"Eleven," corrected Tina as she wrote down the name, "counting that last call."

Luella's face turned purple as she glared at Wendy and Libby. Riley cowered behind them. "I ought to fire you!" she muttered.

"You can't fire us," Wendy shot back. "You're not even paying us!"

"Besides," said Libby, "you read the stories and looked at the pictures before you put them in the paper. You even helped write them."

"Yeah," chimed in Riley. "Anyway, we quit!"

"You can't quit if I already fired you!" hollered Luella, her face a deeper purple.

The office was quiet for a minute as they all stared at each other. Tina sat behind her desk, chin resting on her hands, thinking. She was much calmer than Luella, and Wendy realized that she had seen the editor this way before.

"Luella," said Tina, "when was the last time we got this many calls, bad or good, about a story?"

Luella blinked. "What?"

"We've received thirty-eight phone calls about the fashion

show stories and pictures. More of the callers liked the stories than didn't, and a lot of those who liked what we did were at the show and said we told the story just like it happened. When was the last time we got this many calls about any one thing in the paper?"

"Yeah. How many did you get about that story and picture you ran on road repair equipment?" said Wendy.

This time Tina frowned and shook her head at Wendy. Meanwhile, Luella ran her hands through her hair and shook her head. "I don't know," she muttered. "Wait – yes, I do, too. We got a bunch of calls on our story about the new plastics plant opening."

"Three," corrected Tina. "Two of them wanted to know where they could go to apply for a job. And the third was Mr. Horton. And we should charge him by the phone call. Probably half of the people who called today to cancel were told to call by him, and they will reconsider. I'll bet money on it."

"Don't bet money when I'm not even paying you," Luella growled. Tina looked at Wendy as if trying to tell her something, but Wendy didn't know what. The phone rang again, and Luella grabbed it.

"*Bugle*! Yes, this is the editor. Yes. All right. Yes. They all work here. I just hired them. Of course I'm going to keep them. Thank you. Goodbye!" She banged down the receiver and headed for her office. "Thirty-nine!" she barked over her shoulder to Tina. "Give them an assignment. Just get them out of here!" She stomped into her own office and slammed her door shut.

Tina cleared her throat and took a deep breath, avoiding the eyes of the three new *Bugle* employees. "OK. I have all kinds of story suggestions here from people who called in, just for you three. One woman wanted you to do a story about Roomer.

And, oh, yes, this person called in to suggest you do a story about a sophomore at the high school, whose drawing of a planet won NASA's art competition. Umm, here's a suggestion that you review the Little Theater's new play. The man who called said it's awful and we should warn people before they buy a ten-dollar ticket."

No one said anything. The silence was pulsating. Wendy didn't know about the other two, but she wanted someone to apologize for yelling at her. She liked Tina a lot and felt sorry for her, but she didn't feel the same way about Luella. "I don't feel like doing any stories. Anyway, we're fired, remember?"

"So that's it, huh?" responded Tina. "A few complaints about your work, and you quit? I believed you when you said you wanted to keep the *Bugle* going, but I guess you're not cut out for this business!"

"Not cut out for it? Most of the callers said they liked what we did!"

"So why quit?"

"Apparently not everyone appreciates us," said Wendy.

"Oh, I see. You want everyone to like what you did." Tina shook her head. "Think about that for a minute. Do you think that is ever going to happen? It isn't, not even when you write the truth, and are fair. People don't always want to hear the truth, or don't want to believe you."

"Luella could have been nicer," said Wendy.

Tina busied herself at her desk. "Yes, I know. But you knew what Luella was like before you ever wrote a word. She is not going to change. I don't think she can. Besides, this is the only thing she has ever done, and she has kept this place going by magic. She is desperate to save it. You need to give her a break. And make a decision about what you want to do. I hope you stay because the *Bugle* needs your help. In fact, we need twice as many helpers."

Without speaking, Wendy pulled out the piece of paper from class and handed it to Tina. It had eleven names on it.

"Those are kids in our class who signed up to work here after seeing our story."

"This is great!" said Tina, studying the names. She looked up at the trio, staring at their solemn faces. "But we need all of you, too. So are you quitting?"

"I guess not," muttered Wendy. She looked at Libby and Riley. They both shook their heads "no," but Riley looked uncertain and Libby wouldn't look at anyone.

Wendy sighed. Not only did she have to go home and face her mother's punishment, which had nagged at her all day, but now, thanks to Luella's tantrum, she would have to do some fast talking to get Libby and Riley to stick this out.

"We've got to go, Tina. But there's one name on there – Carmen Degarcia – she wants to do the story on Roomer, mostly on where he went with the hat. No one's seen him since the fashion show, which is really odd since he always hangs around the school. Anyway, we'll be back tomorrow."

"Really?" asked Tina.

Wendy's answer was a nod of her head. She was sure she looked more confident than she felt. No telling what her mother would do to punish her lie.

───── Twelve ─────

Acts of Penance

Outside the *Bugle* office, Wendy wanted to ask Libby and Riley whether they were quitting on her. Combative words were on the tip of her tongue. But something kept her from saying them. She stared at the sidewalk for a moment, then looked at Libby. Libby looked at her.

"So," said Wendy, unnerved by Libby's gaze, "that was strange." No one answered, so her words tumbled out more quickly. "I've made Mom mad enough for one day, so I've got to get home. No telling what she will make me do. How about you guys?"

"Yeah," said Riley. "See you tomorrow."

They split up, all going the same direction by a different route, as if they were strangers who did not want to walk together. Riley kept looking back. Wendy refused to look at him after one glance back and tried not to think about it, which was apparently the same thing her mother was trying to do at home. Everything was the same as usual, with a huge dinner of lasagna, garlic bread, salad and dessert. Except not really the same. They ate at six like they always did, and Wendy helped her father with the dishes, just like she did every night. But the conversations, when there were any, were strained.

"You talked to your mother?" Terry Wright asked Wendy as he rinsed off a plate.

"About…?"

He shrugged. "About anything. She was kind of upset this morning when I left, and I thought she might say something to you. I thought your story was funny, Wendy, but I think she was upset because you lied to her."

"She hasn't said anything to me since this morning," she said.

Her father nodded, but didn't say anything else. Wendy felt like she was an unwanted guest in the house. She waited for something big and bad to happen.

Nothing did until the next morning, as Wendy sat on her wrinkled sheets tying her sneakers. Her mother came in and sat on the window seat facing Wendy, leaning forward with her elbows on her knees. Her mother never leaned forward. Wendy drew back slightly. "I need to talk to you about the *Bugle*," Wanda began.

Wendy held her breath.

"The thought of you working there scares me because I don't like you to be out of my sight for any time at all. It's hard enough for me to let you go to school. That's why I drive you so often, and it's really been a struggle for me to let you ride your bike there. I know this all sounds silly to you, but I think of you as my little girl, and it's difficult to see you grow up." She looked at Wendy and smiled sweetly. It was a smile Wendy hadn't seen in months. She wondered if she should smile back.

"Your father and I talked about the *Bugle* last night. He thought your story was good, and he thinks you can learn a lot by working there. He is in favor of it, as long as it does not interfere with your school work, while I…" she stopped. "I don't like it. I don't see the point, but I know you well enough to know you must have one. So we will let you continue for awhile. I don't suppose you want to quit?" she asked, her voice hopeful, looking at Wendy.

"I didn't think so," she said as Wendy shook her head. "OK. But you have to set things right." Wendy's heart was thumping. Whatever her mother meant by that, it would be big.

"You have to go to both Libby's and Riley's parents and tell them what you three are doing, and you have to make sure they know it was all your idea. And you must apologize to them for your dishonesty and tell them exactly when you are working there and what you do."

Wendy frowned. "But they already know. They saw everything in the paper, just like you and Dad did. And Libby especially won't want me to say anything. Her mother is already upset, and you know Mrs. Weaver."

"I've told you what you have to do," said her mother, getting up. "You need to do it today. Now, do you want a chicken salad sandwich for lunch, or will you eat in the cafeteria?"

Wendy blinked. Her mother was chipping away at her life while giving her a choice for lunch. Didn't she see the absurdity? "Cafeteria's fine," she said, tonelessly.

Her mother nodded and got up, then stopped. "Why is that newspaper so important to you?"

Wendy didn't feel like talking, and nothing she said would matter anyway. She couldn't save the *Bugle* by herself, and she might be the only one left to help after today. Telling her best friends' parents what an untrustworthy person she was would not exactly win her any fans. "No good reason," she responded.

"Make your bed," said Wanda, turning away.

Wendy stared after her, then threw the bedspread across

the bed, grabbed her books, called a goodbye, and was off on her bike before her mother could offer a protest. What would she say to Libby and Riley's parents? Or to Libby and Riley, for that matter? She could just hear their arguments. Libby would say that her mother would never let her out of the house again. Riley might be all right. His parents were different from others, not very worried that he might be getting into mischief. Probably because Riley had never gotten into mischief.

Avoidance was the best solution, she decided, until after she'd told their parents.

Wendy entered the school through a different door. Then she cut first period, hoping this would be a day Mrs. Martino didn't take roll, and if she did, she wouldn't have the office call Wanda. She didn't need more trouble with her mother.

She spent the morning in the girls' restroom, hiding in a stall when someone came in. She also skipped lunch.

The afternoon was easier because she hardly ever saw her friends then anyway. At the end of the school day, she left quickly, again by a different door. She pedaled her bike to a pay phone at a store on Main Street and called Tina at the *Bugle*. "I can't come in today. I have an errand to run," she said.

"Can you come tomorrow?"

"Yes. But I don't know about Libby or Riley."

There was silence on the other end. Finally, Tina said, "I have been calling some of the people on the list you gave me, and we have some other volunteers. But none will be as good as you three."

When Wendy didn't answer, she added, "Carmen is working on the story about Roomer, but I don't think she knows where to look for him. You need to help her."

"OK," said Wendy. "See you tomorrow." She hung up quickly, not that she had to be anywhere. She only knew that she had disappointed Tina and didn't know what else to say. It seemed she would be disappointing a bunch of people before the day was over.

It was only four-thirty, and she knew that neither Riley's parents nor Libby's mother would be home. She went to the city library and sat in the periodical section, going through old issues of the *Bugle* on microfilm. Moffatt Corner had once been a town of twenty thousand people, when the railroad was still a major means of transportation. She pored over photos of downtown, amazed at the railway station crowds. There was a bus depot now where the old train station used to be, and the only trains passing through town these days carried freight instead of people.

She read about one of Moffatt Corner's major crimes in the 1930s, a man stealing a pair of pants from a display in a clothing store. He was chased through town by a crowd that grew at every corner, but he disappeared with the "purloined pants," the story said. She chuckled at the writing, and felt good that the *Bugle* had a long history of covering the town. That was just one more reason it should not close.

At six she reluctantly tore herself away and headed for Riley's house.

It was a warm day, and Mr. Davis was working outside on one of his projects, but Wendy couldn't tell what. The family mutt, a mop-haired dog named Truth, came out to meet her, his whole body wagging as she laid her bike down on the sidewalk. She rubbed his head and stroked his neck for a good minute. "Hi, Mr. Davis," she said finally. So engrossed he was in studying the dozens of small springs and screws and bolts surrounding him on the old quilt on which he sat, cross-legged and barefoot, he hadn't even noticed her arrival.

"Well hello, Wendy," he said, snatching the floppy-brimmed,

faded brown leather hat off his head. His red hair stood up straight like Riley's. He took off his sunglasses and squinted at her, as if he could see better that way. "Riley's inside looking up something for me. I'll get him for you."

"Actually, I need to talk to you," Wendy said. "Am I interrupting something big?" she asked, surveying the dozens of little parts to something that looked like a motor.

"It doesn't matter," he said, shaking his head. "I'm trying to figure out how to air-condition Truth's house before summer. Sheila doesn't want him in the house all summer, so I have to do something. Anyway, I read a magazine article on how to do it, but first I had to recondition this motor I bought several years ago, and now I can't figure out how to get it back together. So I'm just waiting for Riley; he was looking up a diagram. What's on your mind?"

She had rehearsed what to say at least twenty times in her head, and now she couldn't even find the right words to begin. "Hey," said Mr. Davis, interrupting her thoughts, "aren't you working on the *Bugle* with Riley? I think he told me it was all your idea."

"Uh, yes, that's why I'm here. I just wanted to—"

"You know, I'm glad. I think he's going to be a pretty good photographer. He is so bored when he isn't at school. This will give him something new every day. So thanks for including him. I hope you all keep doing it."

"Well, OK," she said. Then she thought about Wanda, who would be checking up. What if Mr. Davis forgot she had come over?

"Mr. Davis? If my mother calls, do you think you and your wife could tell her I came over and told you I was sorry for getting Riley into trouble? And that you thought about it for awhile and decided to let Riley work at the *Bugle* after all?"

He took his sunglasses off again and squinted at her. "Am I supposed to be mad at Riley?"

She nodded. "I think so, and at me. My mother is upset because I lied to her to go to that fashion show and write about it, and she thinks everyone else lied, too. She said I was to tell you I was sorry and it was all my idea."

He nodded thoughtfully. "I will tell her we're not mad anymore, and make sure Sheila knows we're not mad, too."

"OK." Wendy was relieved. "I have to go now! Thanks!"

"Don't you want to wait for Riley? I'm sure he'll be out in just a minute."

"I've got another errand to run, and it's getting kind of late," said Wendy, waving as she pedaled away. But he was already staring at his motor again.

Wendy rode her bike slowly to the Weaver house. She was hoping that Libby and her mother had gone somewhere so she could put this off another day. But Libby answered the door, and she didn't look very happy.

"Where were you today?" she demanded. "I thought you were sick but I called your house and no one answered. You don't look sick."

"I feel kind of sick, but not the way you mean. Is your mom at home?"

"Why?"

Wendy knew she had to tell her now. "Because my mom said I have to apologize to your mom for the lie about what we were doing Saturday morning, and I also have to say that it was all my fault."

"I don't understand," said Libby. "You told your mom that my mom knows everything, didn't you?"

Wendy nodded. "But she said I had to own up to it. That I can't work at the *Bugle* if I don't."

"Where were you today?" Libby asked again.

"I didn't want to tell you what she was making me do because I knew you would be upset. So I avoided you. I was in the restroom all morning, and I skipped lunch."

"Mom's in the kitchen," said Libby, turning away. "Pardon me if I don't go in there with you and watch you screw up my life even more than you already have by bringing all this up again!"

Wendy stood in the doorway alone, unsure about what to do. She struggled to push down whatever was coming up in her throat because she didn't want to throw up in Libby's front yard.

"Libby?" called a musical voice, rhyming the name with tree. "Who is that you are talking to?"

Brigette Weaver had moved to the United States with her parents as a child. Her mother was from Paris, and her father, a captain in the U.S. Air Force, was stationed in France during the second World War and returned there after the war to live for awhile. They met and married, and didn't move to the United States until Brigette was five.

Wendy's mother called Brigette Weaver "reserved," but as far as Wendy was concerned, Mrs. Weaver was just weird. She spoke four languages and traveled to France every spring to visit relatives. She had taken Libby twice. She had moved to Moffatt Corner with her husband because it had been his hometown. When he died suddenly of a heart attack, she stayed there because she hadn't wanted to take Libby away from the only home she had known.

Mrs. Weaver came around the corner and saw Wendy. She stopped suddenly, and Wendy wondered if she was going to tell her to go. But if she was mad enough to send Wendy away, she didn't show it. "Wendy," she said, putting the emphasis on the last syllable, "what are you doing standing in the door? Does Libby not know you are here?"

"I don't think she wants to see me, Mrs. Weaver," said Wendy, looking down at her feet. "I apparently have gotten her into a lot of trouble by getting her to work at the *Bugle*."

Libby had not exaggerated when she said her mother had hit the ceiling. Brigette Weaver started fuming about it again. "Oh, that! My daughter was raised to know better than to write something so...so...mean...And to be so public. It's just not civil. It's barbaric!"

"I just wanted you to know it was my idea, not Libby's," Wendy spoke as quickly as she could.

"Libby has a free will and needs to take responsibility for her own misbehavior," said Mrs. Weaver, her accent growing more pronounced as her face turned red.

"That's true. She has a mind of her own," said Wendy. "But I did push her, and Riley, too. And that's the reason she has been skipping ballet classes, too. She was just..." Wendy stopped, stricken, as she looked at Mrs. Weaver's round eyes. Libby apparently still hadn't told her mother about ballet.

"You have not been going to ballet classes, Libby?" Brigette Weaver called. Libby apparently had been eavesdropping, because she appeared quickly. Her face was white, and she looked at Wendy through accusing eyes.

Brigette Weaver suddenly started speaking in French, the words tumbling out, her voice louder and louder. "What's she saying?" asked Wendy, alarmed, as she paced and gestured wildly.

"She is saying that she doesn't know what will become of me, and that my friends are a horrible influence. Thanks so much for all your help, Wendy. Some friend you are!"

Wendy opened her mouth to protest that she was not a

horrible influence and that she was Libby's friend, but she didn't know whom to address and couldn't find a way to butt in anyway. And before she could utter a word, Libby started speaking French too, facing her mother. She spoke even faster and louder, and gestured even more wildly than her mother. Wendy watched, open mouthed. She didn't know what her friend was saying, but she could guess by her tone that she was not apologizing.

The room was silent when Libby finished speaking. Brigette Weaver, her face pale, stared at her daughter. Then she uttered something and left the room with the two girls staring after her.

"Why did you have to bring up ballet?" Libby demanded. "I thought you were my friend."

"I am your friend. Why do you think I'm here?"

"Because you're selfish! If you were my friend, you wouldn't have come."

"I came to take responsibility for the whole thing," began Wendy.

"Yes. Because it's the only way you could work at that precious newspaper! Did it ever occur to you that what you wanted was not what I wanted?"

Wendy stared, unable to speak.

"Never mind," said Libby. "You'd better go." She opened the door.

"What did your mother say to you?" asked Wendy, turning around in the doorway.

"She called me a juvenile delinquent and said she was washing her hands of me," said Libby, slamming the door.

——— Thirteen ———

A Plan to Find Roomer

Wendy tossed and turned and barely slept. When she did drift into fitful sleep, she relived Libby's front door slamming in her face over and over. In her dream, the door was huge and black, even though the Weavers' front door was a warm cranberry red.

She dreamed that she stood in front of the door for an infinite amount of time, waiting for it to re-open. When she awoke and tried to remember what happened after that, she couldn't. She could only think about the time she met Libby in first grade. They united against a boy who had bullied them both during recess. When they were together, he left them alone. They had never had a serious argument since they were six and had been together a lot.

At breakfast Wendy ate a couple of bites of cereal before excusing herself and pedaling off to school. Even in her sleep-deprived daze she noticed that Wanda said nothing, and Wendy was relieved.

Riley, who was waiting in the schoolyard, wouldn't even look at Wendy when she rode up. He continued to ignore her as she locked her bike in the bike stand at the front of the red brick building and joined him. When she couldn't take the silence any longer, she blurted out an apology.

"Riley, I'm sorry if I made you mad, but I don't know which thing you're mad about. If you will tell me, I'll try to explain it."

He still would not look at her. Eyes focused on his feet, he muttered, "You avoided me all day yesterday, then you come to my house and don't even say hello. How am I supposed to act?"

She was surprised. That one would be easy. She'd done a lot worse things.

"Yes, I should have done that. I knew it as soon as I left there. But I had to speak to your dad, and I was kind of in a hurry after that. I needed to get somewhere else before it got too late."

Riley nodded. "He told me all about it, you owning up to what we did. He didn't care because he didn't think it was a bad thing, but he thought it was nice that you took responsibility."

She felt a little better. "Did he get the motor put back together?"

"It still won't work, but I think I know what's wrong. We'll look at it again today. Where is Libby?"

"I don't know. I had to go to her house after I left yours yesterday. It's why I couldn't wait around to say hello to you."

"Libby didn't know that you were coming by either?"

She shook her head, ashamed that she'd kept this secret from her friends.

"So what happened with Mrs. Weaver?" asked Riley.

"She yelled, and then Libby started yelling. And then I left. Let's just say I've had better days."

"What did they yell?"

"I don't know. It was in French. It was not happy yelling, though. Libby said something about her mother calling her a juvenile delinquent."

"I've never heard Libby yell in French," said Riley.

"Me neither. And for an argument, it sounded pretty good in French. Still, it was pretty awful."

They stood at the entrance for a time, in silence, watching. But when the final bell rang, they headed to first period as a twosome. They didn't mention Libby's absence again, even at lunch. In fact, they were mostly quiet all day. Anything they said to each other seemed strained and unnatural. Still, Riley agreed to go to the *Bugle* office, following Wendy's bike on his own.

Things weren't much better there. Tina was slumped at her desk holding her head in her hands. She looked as if she were about to cry. Then the phone rang, and she waited until the third ring to pick it up. She never waited that long. She listened and said very little before putting it down and looking up at them.

"So you're finally here," she said to them. "Where's Libby?"

"She couldn't come today," said Wendy. "She's sick."

The phone rang again, just as Tina started to speak. She picked it up and listened for a moment before saying, "Yes, I understand. I'm sorry."

"I can't take much more of this," she said, dropping the receiver in its cradle. "We've gotten about two dozen calls today because 'Cheeky and Claude' wasn't in the paper. I can't get any work done because the phone keeps ringing. And Luella just got up and walked out about an hour ago, without saying a word!" She stared at them as if she expected a solution. "This is just not worth it," she added. "I didn't make enough money for this kind of abuse even when Luella was paying me."

"What happened to 'Cheeky and Claude'?" asked Wendy, embarrassed that she hadn't looked for it Wednesday. But then, she didn't get a chance to see the paper until late in the evening, and all she did then was read her story.

"Luella decided to save money by canceling it. It was a dumb thing to do, considering how little she pays for it. But Luella thought no one would notice. She should have to answer the calls herself!"

"We'll take the calls," offered Wendy. "You can take a break, do something else."

Tina nodded, picked up her purse and headed for the door.

"Where are you going?" Wendy asked, alarmed.

"I'm taking a break, like you said."

"I didn't mean you should leave! I meant you should get some work done!"

Gripping her purse tightly under her arm, Tina was almost out the door. Suddenly, she turned around. "If Luella doesn't come back, you two lock the front door when you leave. Oh…Carmen will be by today. She's still trying to find Roomer. She must have made ten phone calls yesterday trying to track him down. You two will have to help her before she gets discouraged and quits. And Burnam Horton came by to volunteer. It didn't occur to me that he would be one of your volunteers, Wendy, and I think we ought to steer clear of him, given who his father is. He seemed kind of unpleasant. But overall your list looks good. I'm about halfway through calling people on it."

"Burnam Horton volunteered?" asked Wendy, stunned.

But Tina was already gone. Wendy and Riley stared at each

other. "Why would he volunteer?" Wendy asked Riley. "He hates the *Bugle*."

Then the phone rang.

"You get it," said Wendy. Riley's eyes were wide as he stared at the phone, his freckles popping out as his face went pale. "Never mind!" said Wendy as she grabbed it. "*Bugle*! Yes, I read 'Cheeky and Claude.' Yes, it was a mistake. It will be back the next issue. You're welcome."

"Why did you say that?" demanded Riley as she hung up the phone. "You don't know that it will be back. Even Tina didn't say that to people who called."

Wendy shrugged. "Too bad. That's what she should do, and if she doesn't, I won't be here to answer the phones. Luella can do it herself."

"Do what myself?" growled a voice behind them, startling them both so badly they almost fell from their chairs. "And where's Tina?"

"You should announce yourself when you're coming in the back!" said Wendy, trying to recover her composure. "Tina was sick of answering the phones. People apparently have been calling all day asking what happened to 'Cheeky and Claude,' and then you left and she got mad. So she left too, and put us in charge. We're telling people who call that they will be back in the next issue."

Luella glared at her, but Wendy wouldn't look away even though her heart was pounding. "And why would you say that?" rasped Luella.

"Because it was the right thing to do," said Wendy, hating how pious she sounded. Then she heard another voice speaking.

"Nobody told us what to do," said Riley. "But then, nobody was here but us. See, it's important if you run a place that you actually stick around to run it and not just leave people who work for you without any instructions. Saying 'Cheeky and Claude' will be back next issue just makes the most sense, especially when your readers are demanding it. So that is what's going to happen, right?"

Wendy stared at him. The color had come back to his face. He hadn't stammered once. He spoke with such confidence, in fact, that she didn't see how Luella could disagree.

"Thank you, Mr. Davis, for your homily on how to run a business. It will be difficult for a slow-witted person like me, but I will try. Now…" Luella stopped as the door opened and Carmen walked in. Wendy and Riley greeted her, and Luella stared at her for a moment before returning to what she'd been saying. "I am sure you have other things to do, so why don't you do them? I will answer the phones."

"Luella Cathcart, meet Carmen Degarcia, one of your new reporters," said Wendy. "Tina gave her an assignment, and we need to work with her on that. You sure you know what to say to callers?"

"I think I can figure it out!" snapped Luella.

Tina's phone rang again, and Wendy pulled Carmen away from the desk. Riley followed a few steps behind. "Who is that grump?" whispered Carmen. "She was here yesterday, too!"

"That's the editor," said Wendy.

"Oh. I thought she'd be…taller."

"She's taller behind her own desk, when she's yelling at you," said Wendy. "Have you had any luck finding Roomer?"

"No. It's like he's just vanished."

"I think he's around," said Wendy. "I can't explain it, but I have that feeling."

The three of them decided to look for the dog on foot at all the places they knew he went, including the bakery on Main

Street and Otto's, where Otto Brinker, the owner, saved him bones and scraps from the meat he cut up. They also searched the streets right around the middle school where he stayed at night.

After an hour of fruitless searching, they all had to go home, but no one wanted to give up. "I didn't think reporting would be this hard," said Carmen.

Wendy suggested they go back to the *Bugle* office to see if Luella was still there. "Maybe she can give us some suggestions about what to do."

Riley rolled his eyes, but didn't say anything.

"The grump? I don't know…" said Carmen.

"She has experience in these things. We should at least ask her, unless one of you has a better idea."

So back to the office they went, and Luella was still at Tina's desk. She was putting down the phone when they walked in. Wendy was certain it had rung continuously since they'd left. This would be a good education for Luella.

"Back so soon?" she asked.

While Riley and Carmen cowered behind her, Wendy stepped to the desk. "We need some advice."

"Do I look like Ann Landers?"

"This is important," said Wendy impatiently. "We're trying to find Roomer. You know, the dog that stole the hat? He's disappeared, but I don't think he's really gone. I think he's trapped somewhere. What do you think we should do?"

"What makes you think he's not dead?"

Wendy's stomach turned over. She hadn't allowed herself to think about that more than a moment, and she wasn't ready to give up yet. "He might be, but I don't think so. What have you done before when you can't find someone?"

"I put out a trial balloon and see what happens," said Luella.

"What's a trial balloon?"

Luella turned to the computer on Tina's desk and began typing. Her fingers flew over the keyboard. After a minute or two, she clicked on the print button and told Wendy to get what was coming out of the printer and read it out loud.

"Where is Roomer?" read Wendy. "That's the headline," she said to Carmen and Riley. Then she continued reading. "Roomer, the dog who stole the show and a hat at Saturday's Easter fashion show has disappeared. Students from Riddle Middle School, where Roomer lives, have missed him since Monday, when they returned to school but he didn't.

"He's disappeared, but I don't think he's really gone," said Wendy Wright, one of the middle school students and the *Bugle* reporter who covered the fashion show and reported on Roomer's antics.

Wendy looked up from the story to Luella. "I get it. We add details about all the places we've looked."

Luella nodded. "We put the story on the front page and include a phone number for people to call if they've spotted him. We'll give them the number of the answering machine. We probably will get a bunch of tips. You ready to finish it?"

They all nodded, and gathered around Luella at the keyboard and offered suggestions. She took each idea and turned it into a proper sentence. They finished the story in about ten minutes.

"Good work," said Luella. "It goes in the next edition, above the fold. I'm going to print some fliers, too, and put them in a few places around town. So you'll need to come in and check the answering machine tomorrow so it doesn't get too full."

By the time the three of them returned the next day, Tina looked much better. She grinned as they walked in. "That answering machine is blinking like crazy. I haven't had a chance to touch it, so I am glad you're here. I hope it's full of tips about Roomer. By the way, Luella said 'Cheeky and Claude' will be back Saturday. You two have any idea how that happened?"

Wendy shrugged. "You'd better ask Luella. I really don't know."

She started to ask Tina what she had told Burnam Horton when he volunteered, but just then the phone rang, and the call tied Tina up for several minutes. Wendy's question would have to wait for another time.

—— Fourteen ——

A Whispered Tip

Wendy got a notebook and pencil and sat down at the answering machine. Riley and Carmen leaned over the machine, elbows on the desk, on either side of her.

"Ready?" she asked. They nodded, and she waved her hands in the air dramatically, as if she were conducting an orchestra, before pressing "Play." The first three calls were hangups, and the fourth and fifth were from a young woman who wanted Pizza Palace and obviously didn't know the number. "This is weird," said Riley. "It appears that most people don't know how to use the telephone."

The next call was a man who wanted the *Bugle* to quit "playing around" with "Cheeky and Claude" and not leave it out anymore. "I've been a subscriber to this paper for twelve and a half years, and 'Cheeky and Claude' is my favorite feature. If you leave it out again, I might have to come down there and straighten you out!"

Tina started to giggle.

Wendy rolled her eyes. "Maybe this was not a great idea after all."

With the next call, a hush fell over the four of them, and the hair stood up on the back of Wendy's neck. She thought the voice was young, but could not be sure because it was whispering. "I know where your dog is," the voice hissed. "He's tied up in the back yard at 4030 Weeping Willow Lane, and he's not doing very well. I think you need to get him very soon."

Wendy glanced at Riley, then at Carmen. "Did something about the voice sound familiar to you?" she asked them.

"Yes, but it wasn't the voice. It was the way he said the words," said Riley.

"So you thought it was a boy, too?" Wendy asked. Riley nodded.

"Play it again," suggested Carmen. "I've heard something like that before but I can't place it."

Wendy pressed the rewind button and then "Play." In a moment the voice was hissing at them again. This time, Wendy wrote down the address. "Do you have one of those books that lets you look up who lives at a certain address?" she asked Tina, who nodded and pulled a large, hard-backed orange book out of a drawer of her desk and handed it to Carmen, who gave it to Wendy.

As Wendy paged through until she found Weeping Willow Lane, Riley rewound the answering machine again and replayed the message.

"Here's Weeping Willow," announced Wendy, then ran her finger down the addresses silently as Riley held up his hand for quiet. He played the message a third time. He pushed the stop button just as Wendy found the address and slid her finger over to the name beside it. She gasped, and she and Riley said the name simultaneously: "Burnam Horton!"

"Yes!" cried Carmen. "You're right! That's who it is!"

"Of course," said Tina. "Remember, I told you he came here to volunteer. But he wasn't on your list."

"Burnam Horton hates the *Bugle,*" said Wendy. "I don't know what he was doing here. You're sure he came by to volunteer?"

Tina nodded. "That's what he said. He was nervous, too, about coming in. It was like he thought I would chase him out. I don't really want him here, but I tried to be nice to him. I just told him to come back next week. I wanted to talk to you first, just to see if maybe you had sent him. I guess you didn't."

Wendy shook her head.

"Why would Roomer be tied in the back yard at his address?" asked Riley.

"Someone there probably went hunting for him after he stole Mrs. Horton's hat," said Wendy. "I bet it was Mr. Horton!" She closed her eyes, not wanting to think about what he would do to the dog. Burnam wearing long-sleeved shirts even in hot weather flashed through her mind.

"But why would Burnam call about it?" asked Carmen. "That's not his style."

"No," agreed Wendy. "But he actually sounded worried about the dog. Maybe Roomer's hurt bad and he's afraid of what will happen." Her stomach felt queasy.

"It's got to be a trick!" exclaimed Riley. "Burnam doesn't do good deeds!"

"I think it's for real," Wendy said. "He whispered it so that we would not know it was him. We have to get over there. Tina, can you drive us?"

"Sure, as soon as Luella gets back from making her ad calls. I can't leave unless someone else is here because we have a truck coming with a load of paper, and somebody's got to be here to unlock the warehouse door."

Wendy nodded, rose and hooked her book bag straps over her shoulders. She looked at Riley, and he did the same. Carmen got up, too.

"We've got to get over there now," said Wendy, heading for the door. "See you later."

"Just a minute, you three." Tina spoke in the quiet, commanding tone of voice of a parent or teacher. Wendy stopped, as did the other two who'd been right on her heels. "Say you even know where 4030 Weeping Willow is. Say you go over there and find the dog. Just what do you think you are going to do then?"

"Untie him," said Wendy, shrugging. "Take him to a vet, if he needs one."

"So you're going to trespass on private property. What if you get caught? And by the way, there is no vet in Moffatt Corner."

"That means someone who can drive will have to take us to Marlett," said Wendy.

"I will drive you all over the countryside if you will just wait!" Tina said, her voice rising.

"This can't wait," said Wendy.

Tina reached for Wendy's arm. "Luella will be back very soon, and one of us will go with you," she said, pleading this time instead of instructing. "You need one of us with you. Please, just wait." She heard a loud engine and glanced out the murky front window. "See, here's the truck right now. I need to go unlock the back. As soon as he is through unloading, I'll lock up the office and go. Fifteen minutes at the most."

"OK," said Wendy, plopping into the nearest chair, and the other two sat, too. They waited patiently as Tina got her keys and headed to the warehouse. As soon as she was gone, as if in mental communication with each other, they got up simultaneously and slipped out the front door.

"She'll be mad," said Riley.

"I know, but she won't even know we're gone for fifteen minutes," said Wendy.

"Do you know where to go?" asked Carmen.

Wendy nodded. "It's a fancy new subdivision on the edge of town. It won't take long to get over there. Just follow me."

Eight minutes and a few seconds later, they coasted past 4030 Weeping Willow, an imposing red brick colonial house with an ornate glass front door. While other lawns showed signs of emerging from late spring, the lawn at 4030 was emerald, probably the greenest in the whole subdivision. The mailbox at the end of the curving sidewalk was brightly polished brass with black letters spelling out "The Hortons" in fancy script. Red and white flowers lined both sides of the walkway, which was swept clean, not even a blade of grass or a speck of dirt apparent.

As she stared at the house, one of Wendy's fears was realized. The house was smack in the middle of the block, so you couldn't even see the back yard from the street. When she moved to one side of it, she could see a privacy fence and that was all. It was higher than any neighboring fence, she guessed eight feet.

She pedaled down the street as if she lived there. Motioning the others to follow, she went around the corner to the next street, Red Oak, where the houses backed up to Weeping Willow. Counting the houses, she stopped in front of the fourth and tried to peer into the back yard. The Horton's house had to back up to this one or the one next door.

As she straddled her bicycle, pondering, Riley eased up beside her, then Carmen, until they were three abreast. "Which one backs up to the Horton house, do you think?" she asked Riley.

He looked from one to the other. "Both of them," he said finally. "See the slate roof back there? That's the Horton's roof. The house is so big, it takes up as much room as both of these."

She knew they couldn't linger in the street long. Three kids on bicycles in this neighborhood were going to stand out. The Neighborhood Watch people probably allowed kids outside at certain times and made them promise they wouldn't yell or loiter.

She pedaled off, motioning again for the others to follow. She'd seen a small neighborhood park nearby, and that's where she headed. Once there, she laid her bike on the grass and then sat down beside it, cross-legged. The other two did the same until they were sitting in a circle, heads down.

"Here's what I'm thinking," she said, and talked for a moment. The other two were silent, listening.

"I can do that," said Carmen.

"I don't like it," said Riley. "What if they say no? And if they say yes, then what?"

"I already told you – that's where you and Carmen come in."

"I just don't like it," said Riley.

"You have a better idea?" asked Wendy.

He shook his head.

"Then we'd better get on with it," she said.

——— Fifteen ———

A Lie Told in French

They climbed back onto their bikes, Riley a bit more reluctantly than the other two, and made a circle down Weeping Willow, then around the corner to Red Oak. They stopped again in front of 4025 Red Oak.

"Ready?" Wendy asked the other two as she dismounted from her bicycle and left it on the curb. "I doubt our bikes will get stolen here."

"What happens if we find Roomer?" asked Riley. "Are we going to lift a fifty-pound dog over an eight-foot fence? "

"I don't know, Riley. Sometimes you just have to go with the flow, you know?"

"Now is no time to talk in stupid rhymes, Wendy."

"I am not trying to act stupid. The rhyme just happened. But it's exactly what I mean. If Roomer is there, something will occur to us. We have to find out."

Wendy led the way up the sidewalk, trying to stroll casually. When they were all three gathered on the veranda, a large covered area with sparkling white wicker chairs, tables, ottomans, cushioned sofas, and dozens of potted plants, Wendy pressed the doorbell. After a minute, a uniformed, dark-haired woman in her twenties opened the door and looked at them, a question mark on her face. When she spoke, Wendy's heart sank.

"Oui?" she said.

"Oh, boy." Wendy searched her brain for the right words. "Parlez-vous Englais?"

"How'd you know to say that?" said Riley, as the dark-haired woman shook her head.

"I don't remember. A book Miranda had, I guess...you think she'd understand hand signals?"

He shrugged, then Carmen moved up to the door and said "Se habla Espanol?"

"You speak Spanish?" Riley asked. "Si. Of course," said Carmen. "That was my first language. English is my second."

But it didn't matter. The woman was shaking her head again and seemed a bit anxious. She gave them a half wave, then backed away and shut the door.

"I feel like I'm in the Twilight Zone," said Riley. "I'm the only one who doesn't know another language."

They stood in front of the door for a moment, Wendy staring at Riley. "I know someone who will speak to you, though, who probably won't speak to me. And she also speaks French."

Riley stared at her thoughtfully. "You really think she'd do it? I mean, she barely speaks to me, and she hasn't even looked at you since you went to her house and upset her mother."

"We have to at least ask, Riley. Do you know anyone else who speaks French?"

"Yeah. Her mother. It might be just as easy to ask her."

"Who are you talking about?" asked Carmen, and Wendy told her.

"Libby Weaver speaks French? But I thought you two were best friends," she said to Wendy. "Why won't she speak to you?"

"It's a long story. Let's just say I got her into big trouble with her mother."

"If she will talk to Riley, then what are we waiting for? We need to get her over here."

Wendy saw a curtain move on the window next to the door. "We'd better not stand here any longer, or the maid might call the police."

"That's OK," said Riley as they headed down the front walk. "I feel sure no officer in Moffatt Corner speaks French."

They rode their bicycles around the neighborhood until they found a pharmacy and grocery store on a busy street. A pay phone sign hung above a small booth outside. Between them, they came up with the right change. "What's the number?" Riley asked Wendy.

She dictated it, he repeated it, then she and Carmen retreated and watched.

"He's talking to someone," said Carmen.

"Let's hope he gets Libby and not her mother. She might not let Libby talk to him."

"Look!" said Carmen. "He's motioning to you to come!"

Wendy couldn't believe Libby actually wanted to talk to her. She trudged to the phone, in no great hurry because she didn't know what to say. Riley put his hand over the receiver.

"I told her the story and asked her to come over, but she wants to talk to you first," he said.

Wendy breathed deeply and took the phone. "Libby?" she said. "It's Wendy."

There was silence for a long moment, but Libby was there. Wendy could hear her breathing. "I can't believe you are doing this," Libby said finally. "Do you know my mother is talking about putting me in a private Catholic school in Marlett? I would

125

not know one single soul over there!"

"Tell her you won't go," said Wendy, her voice quiet.

"Oh, just like that, huh? You saw her the other day! How far do you think I would get with that?"

"You might have to say it more than once. What's 'no' in French?"

There was another silence, then Wendy thought she heard a giggle. She'd almost decided she was hearing things when she heard it again. And again.

"It's 'non.' I could say it in English and repeat it in French," Libby sputtered.

Wendy started laughing, too, feeding off her friend's mirth. Soon she was laughing so hard she was shaking and her eyes were watering, and she could tell Libby was as well. Riley looked at her round-eyed, which made her laugh even harder. Finally, the giggles petered out, and Wendy wiped her eyes.

"Where are you?" asked Libby.

"At the corner of Old West Avenue and Tenth Street, right at the edge of the Hidden Hills subdivision."

"OK," said Libby. "I'll be there in a few minutes."

"You sure?"

"I'm not grounded, if that's what you mean. My mother doesn't believe in grounding me. She just yells."

"Be careful," said Wendy, then she hung up.

"What was the joke?" asked Riley.

"You kind of had to be there, or it isn't so funny. But she is on her way."

"She forgave you just like that? I can't believe it," he said. "I thought it might take a year or so for her to talk to you again."

"I'm not sure she was really mad at me, Riley," said Wendy.

Libby pedaled into the parking lot less than ten minutes later, wearing a simple white T-shirt and jeans. She smiled shyly

at Carmen. "How did you get roped into this?" she asked her.
"It's part of being a volunteer at the *Bugle*," said Carmen.

They gathered around Libby and told her what had happened and what they wanted her to say to the maid. "You think she will go for it?" Libby asked.

"It's the only idea we have at the moment," said Wendy.

"And assuming we find Roomer in that yard, then what? How do we get him out of there?"

Riley flashed Wendy a triumphant look. "Exactly my thoughts. But she hasn't gotten that far in her plan yet."

"Look, Riley, do you have any ideas?" fumed Wendy.

Libby held up her hands. "It's OK. Let's not fight. We're all on the same side, remember? Let's just go over there and see if Roomer is there, and if he is, we can figure out what to do."

So they headed for 4025 Red Oak again, single file, Wendy in the lead. Once there, they laid their bikes down at the curb a second time. This time, Carmen suggested she and Riley wait there and let Wendy and Libby return to the door. "She'd be more nervous facing four of us than two. If she agrees to let us do it, you two can signal us, and we'll join you."

They agreed that was a good idea, and Wendy and Libby headed for the door. "I'm glad you called me," said Libby. "I've missed you and Riley."

"Same here. I'm just sorry for the trouble I caused you."

Libby shrugged. "It wasn't your fault. The smallest thing can set my mom off."

"She's really thinking about sending you to school in Marlett?"

"She's talking about it. But I'm just going to tell her 'non'," said Libby, with a wide grin, looking sideways at Wendy.

They were at the door, and Wendy pressed the bell. "You know what to say, right?"

Libby nodded. "I tell her that we lost our soccer ball in the back yard and ask her if we can go get it."

The maid didn't seem all that happy to see two children at the door again, nor at all surprised that they'd brought someone who could speak her language. But she and Libby talked animatedly for a few minutes, with lots of gestures. To Wendy, it sounded as if they were bargaining. She chewed on the side of her mouth and grew more impatient with each breath, wondering why French was considered a romance language.

The maid regarded both of them thoughtfully, then pointed to Libby and said something in French. "She wants me to go by myself," Libby told Wendy.

"I don't think you ought to do that. Somebody needs to get over the fence. I thought Riley might could climb it."

Libby said something else to the woman, pointing to Wendy, then to herself. The maid hesitated, then said, "Oui."

"Merci," Libby said to her, turning to Wendy. "OK. She said you and I can go. The gate's around that way," Libby said, pointing to the driveway. "And we need to go now, before she changes her mind."

"We need to tell Riley and Carmen."

Libby shook her head. "They can't go. It looks like one of us will be climbing the fence."

"We need to tell them, at least," said Wendy.

But Libby was already trotting around the side of the house. "There's no time," she called. The maid might change her mind at any minute. She was awfully nervous about this."

So they hurried to a large heavy gate with a metal latch that was difficult to maneuver. When Wendy figured out how to press the latch, the gate swung open and she stepped inside. She stood there, gazing at the huge area, and felt like a gnat in a forest. The back edge of the yard appeared miles away, and in between was a canopy of well-trimmed oaks, each one land-scaped with leafy purple flowering plants. The centerpiece was a large fountain made of rocks, gurgling peacefully, fronds of water-loving plants surrounding the water, the tips of their leaves gracefully breaking the surface.

Just behind Wendy, a tiled veranda looked out onto the park-like lawn. Here lounged more sofas and chairs of glistening white wicker. A few red geraniums in huge pots provided dashes of color.

As Wendy's eyes swept the lawn a second time, she spotted the rectangular swimming pool in one corner. But she was most interested in the ladder that led up to the diving board.

"Look," she said to Libby, who was also gazing open-mouthed at the scene before her. "The ladder is positioned perfectly for me to look in both back yards from one spot. Can you tell if the maid is watching us?"

"I don't know. She could be anywhere in that house. Let's scour the yard as if we're looking for our ball. I'll go to one corner, you go to the other. You can work your way over to the ladder."

Wendy nodded, and was surprised to find how easy it was to pretend there was really a soccer ball nestled somewhere in the giant park of a yard. She peered behind the red geraniums and looked carefully through the purple plants around several oaks. She circled the fountain and wished she could spend some time sitting on the rocks, dipping her hand into the water.

All the while she drew closer to the ladder, and finally, she was at its base.

"I'm going up the ladder," she said to Libby, who had joined her. "I feel like the maid is watching us. If she comes out, tell her that I'm looking to see if the ball is in one of these other yards." Wendy held her breath and quickly climbed.

She was on the top step, twisting around to see behind her just as the young woman rushed from the house yelling something in French. Libby started yelling, too, but Wendy couldn't tell what she was saying because she wasn't listening. She was staring at Roomer, below and to her right. He was tied to a short iron stake with a rope only a couple of feet long. He appeared to be skin and bones as he reclined on dead grass. Everything in this yard was dead, from the trees, to what had once been flowers, to the grass. It was a stark contrast to the yard Wendy was in as well as to its own front yard.

Roomer appeared to have sores on his front legs. She knew it was him because she could see the scar near his left ear, across the top of his head.

"Roomer!" she called. After a moment, he slowly raised his head tried to wag his tail, which thumped pitifully against the ground, then stopped. Then he rested his head on his paws as if too tired to do much more. "Sit tight, boy. I'm coming."

Wendy couldn't have told anyone how she got from the ladder to the fence, but somehow, leaning at a crazy angle, she grabbed the fence with her right hand, then her right leg, then her left. She had to climb up a bit before she could go over. She ignored the splinters in her hands and the scrapes on her arms as she struggled over the top.

Clambering down the fence boards on the other side was like slipping down a hill with a dead-man's incline. Only a few inches down, she felt her toes slip off the smooth boards. There was nothing for her hands to grip. Her stomach lurched into her chest as she fell, and she felt the prickly heat on her arms and neck that told her something bad was going to happen.

Her right leg hit the ground first, then her head bumped something. Then everything went black. Right before that, she could have sworn she heard Riley yelling something.

──── Sixteen ────

Tasseled Shoes

Her eyes saw the tasseled, polished brown shoes on the dead grass first, and she pondered on them a moment. They were the shoes of someone who cared about shoes, perhaps more than people. They were glossy and without scuff marks.

The shoes and tassels seemed misplaced standing on dead grass, like a big shiny bow on disheveled gray hair.

She tried to lift her head so she could see more than shoes, but she couldn't, so she let only her eyes, which were having trouble focusing, move. Up, up, beyond the brown pants and white shirt, way up, into the cold, dark eyes of a man she knew immediately even though she'd never met him before.

When their eyes met, he spoke. At the sound of his gravelly voice, she felt the prickly heat again.

"It looks like you have discovered my secret. Roomer lives with me now. You can see how well he's doing." He smiled. Wendy thought of a barracuda.

She could not find her voice. She tried to move again, harder this time, but pain shot through her upper left torso and her right leg. Her head throbbed. She craned her neck enough to see the crazy way her right leg was positioned beneath her. It looked all wrong, but she couldn't figure out why.

"Get up!" commanded the man. When she didn't move, he reached for her arm with slender, cold fingers and pulled.

She yelped as pain shot through her. "Don't!" she cried, but her voice sounded odd.

Roomer, who had scooted on his belly as close to Wendy as his short rope would allow, growled. One of the brown tasseled shoes moved quickly to kick him in the side. The blow landed on him with a sickening thud. His yelp made Wendy even sicker.

With the one hand she could move, Wendy grabbed the man's ankle. Though the pain almost blinded her, she hung onto it as he tried to shake it off and lost his balance and almost fell backward, cursing.

"You let go or you'll get worse than the dog!" he said through clenched teeth. But she wouldn't. As he regained his balance, he reached down again for her arm, and she winced as his big hand closed around it.

She watched the hand as if through a piece of nylon net and wondered if this were truly happening. This was not how she pictured the rescue of Roomer at all, not one bit. She couldn't remember how she'd gotten into this particular fix. The last memory she had in her head was going through a massive gate into someone's lush back yard. She wished she was still there.

She wondered where her body would be found, and she wanted to tell her parents she was sorry. The man yanked her arm again, but she didn't have the heart to get Roomer in trouble, so she gritted her teeth and remained silent. A tear trickled down her cheek.

Then a voice crackled through the dead back yard and if it hadn't been for her pain, Wendy would have thought she was dreaming.

"Is that how you treat an injured child, Horton? Get your hands off her and do not touch her again!"

The man jerked his hand away as if he'd been burned. "You're trespassing on private property! Get outta my yard," he growled.

"Interesting, you pointing out what's right and wrong. Back away from her," said the voice, sounding like a cop. Maybe it was a cop. The tasseled shoes moved away from Wendy.

Then she heard sirens and saw her mother's face hovering detached, high above hers. Then it moved closer and closer and smiled, and Wendy decided it was an angel's face. Cool dream, she thought. She didn't have that many dreams where she got her mother mixed up with a beautiful angel.

Then her mother's hand touched her forehead and her arm, and Wendy smelled her perfume, and she decided it all might be real. "The ambulance is coming to get you Wendy. You are going to be just fine…do you hear me?"

"Are you mad at me again?" asked Wendy, but it sounded like "R ooo hatamee aneen?" Her mother or the angel must have understood, though. The smile widened and the head moved from side to side in a "no." The smooth, cool hand continued to stroke her face.

Then a bunch of faces appeared – Luh…luh…a person who's name began with L. And Riley, Carmen and Tina. And a woman in a uniform, babbling, who looked vaguely familiar. Wendy went back to the first face, the one whose name began with an L, and tried to remember the name. She really liked this face. The woman in the uniform babbled softly to her, and the L-face answered. They both smiled at Wendy, who tried to smile back.

All of them hovered above her. The cop had the tall man with the glossy tasseled shoes cornered, away from everyone else. She was yelling at him, but the words sounded foreign, and she wasn't in a police uniform, but in a sweatshirt and jeans. Then Wendy realized it was Luella Cathcart.

"I didn't know Luella could speak French, too," she said, but that's not what it sounded like, and no one understood. She looked a little further to the side, as far as she could make her eyes go, and she saw a small figure squatting by Roomer, stroking his ears. It looked like…she blinked…it was B-B-Burnam Horton. He was untying the dog.

"You leave that dog where it is!" growled the man with brown tasseled shoes. But Burnam kept on doing what he was doing, as if no one had said anything.

Then there were two men and a woman that Wendy didn't know hovering above her, and all the other faces moved away. One of the women was talking to her, asking her questions. "Do you know your name?"

"It's Wendy, Wendy Wright," she heard Riley say, and the person whose name she couldn't say shushed him.

"What he shaid," Wendy told the woman – or thought she did. The woman wore a crisp white shirt with some sort of emblem on it, and dark blue pants and athletic shoes with dark trim. "But can you say it for me?" asked the woman, smiling slightly.

"Wundy Lucee-ul White. Ooh can caw me Wucy."

"Do you know what day it is, Lucy?"

"Fri...Fri... My ead urts."

"Don't close your eyes, Lucy! Look at me. Can you see how many fingers I'm holding up?"

"Dunchu ave to be able to count to do dis job?" asked Wendy.

The woman smiled again. "How many fingers?" she asked.

"Twee. Ou ave nice nails."

"Thank you, Lucy." She looked over her shoulder at her companions who had been doing things in the background while she was asking Wendy questions. "Are you ready?" she asked them. Then she turned back to Wendy. "We're going to move you on the stretcher now, and it's going to hurt. But not for long. OK?" She patted Wendy's arm and got up.

And then Wendy felt herself almost floating in the air as several pairs of hands shifted her twisted body off the ground onto another surface. Pain seared her side and leg like a hot poker, and she winced. But she didn't say anything.

"Lucy, can you tell me where it hurts?" the woman asked.

Because whatever she said sounded stupid, Wendy pointed to her right leg, her left side and her head.

"OK, let's go!" said the woman, and Wendy felt herself rising in the air. Through her blurry eyes, she got a better picture of everyone there. She stared at them and they stared back at her. No one was doing anything about Roomer.

"Wait!" she wanted to say, but nothing would come out of her mouth, and the pain in her head was so bad that she just wanted to go to sleep. Maybe if she closed her eyes just for a moment, the pain would go away. As she let them close, the woman in charge said, "Lucy, open your eyes! Lucy!"

She tried, but they would not open. Then she heard someone, the girl whose face she liked but whose name she couldn't remember, say, "Her name isn't Lucy. She just told you that as a joke. Her name is Wendy."

The woman in charge said something to the others that Wendy couldn't understand – lots of people in Moffatt Corner apparently spoke French – and then she knew they were moving, fast. Somewhere in the darkness of her head hung the questions she hadn't been able to ask: "What about Roomer? What about Burnam? Where was she and where were they taking her? What was Luella saying to the man with brown tasseled shoes? Was that Burnam's father? If so, what about Burnam?"

Someone was holding her hand and didn't let it go, even when the bed she was on slid into the ambulance. Although her eyes would not open, she smelled her mother's perfume.

"Wendy. Wendy!" she heard someone say. But she couldn't answer, and slipped into darkness.

Seventeen

Nylon Net Days

Her sleep was the kind that wasn't really sleep, where her eyes would drift open and she'd discover she was in a strange place. Then her eyes would drift shut again before she could find out where she was. But she wasn't really asleep, because she could hear people saying things. Then her eyes would be open again, this time when a light was shining in them, and someone was asking questions. And she would try to answer, but the words wouldn't come out because something was wrong with her mouth.

This happened over and over again.

Each time she woke she glanced around the room briefly. It was always the same unfamiliar room swathed in nylon net. She didn't know where she was or why she was here, but recognized some of the faces around her. Her mother and father were there, and Libby and Riley. Carmen was there once, with Tina and Luella.

One time she heard a new voice and opened her eyes to see Mrs. Martino, who was talking to someone. "Hello," Wendy said weakly, and a neck craned around Mrs. Martino to have a look. She couldn't be sure through the nylon net, but she thought it was Burnam.

"What are you…" Then a nurse came in the room and said something to them. Mrs. Martino said, "Sorry we didn't get to talk, but we'll try to come back. Goodbye, Wendy," and the person she thought was Burnam gave a little salute and tried to smile. She decided then she was dreaming. As far as she knew, Burnam never smiled. And why would he go anywhere with Mrs. Martino?

When she saw a face she knew, she wanted to ask what day it was and where she was and if Roomer was OK, but she couldn't put the words together. When she slept, she dreamed she was running through a field of yellow flowers with Roomer at her side, or racing down Main Street on her bike. Once she dreamed about brown tasseled shoes kicking Roomer and tried hard to wake up. She felt someone's hand on her shoulder, shaking her.

"Lucy! Lucy! Wake up!"

She opened her eyes. She didn't know the face in front of her own. "You were groaning in your sleep," said the woman. "Are you in pain?"

"My head hurts, but that's all. Is today still Thursday?" she croaked. "What happened to me?"

The woman smiled and said, "I can understand you now. I couldn't for awhile. How are you?"

"My head hurts. Who is Lucy?"

"Don't you know?" asked the woman.

Wendy shook her head.

"What is your name?"

"Wendy Wright." She watched the woman turn the pages of a chart, but Wendy wasn't very interested. She was more concerned about getting something to drink. But she didn't have the energy to talk much and doubted the stranger would care anyway. With effort she asked, "Is it Thursday? Why am I here? What happened to me?"

"I'll get someone for you," said the woman, who glided from the room.

"Get someone who knows what day it is," muttered Wendy, as her left hand went up to her head to feel if there were bandages on it. It was a small movement, but it sent pain radiating up her side. "Ow!" she cried, just as another woman entered. "I guess I'm not supposed to move," she said, wincing.

"Some movement is good for you, although you won't be running any races for awhile. How are you feeling?"

"My head hurts, and I'm tired. But I don't know why. Every time I wake up, I am in this bed. What day is it?"

"It's a bright and beautiful Saturday afternoon, Wendy. I am Dr. Pamela Morgan."

"Saturday!" exclaimed Wendy. "What happened to Thursday?"

Dr. Pamela was silent as Wendy looked around her. A shelf on one wall was full of pots and vases of pretty yellow flowers. On a window sill, irises, daffodils, tulips and some kind of flower Wendy didn't recognize were crowded together. A stack of creamy envelopes teetered on the small metal bedside table. The top one had her name scrawled on it. She had a thousand questions and didn't know which one to ask first.

Almost as if she was reading her mind, Dr. Morgan said, "Your friends told me to tell you as soon as you woke up that Roomer is recuperating at Riley's house, and that…let me see if I can say this right. That Luella made sure Burnam would be OK. Does any of that make sense to you?"

Wendy nodded. She smiled at the thought of Roomer at

Riley's house. Mr. Davis had probably made him a special heated bed. Roomer would be fine, and that made her feel better. She knew the dog had something to do with her being in this strange place, although she could not remember what.

But her mind couldn't understand the message about Burnam. "What was the last part of what you said?"

"That Luella made sure Burnam would be OK. You don't know what that means?"

Wendy frowned as she tried to remember. A vague memory came into her head about Burnam stroking Roomer, and about Burnam in this room, craning his neck around Mrs. Martino to see her. She seemed to recall thinking he was in danger, but try as she might, she could not make the pieces of the puzzle fit together. She sighed and looked around the room again. At least the nylon net was gone. She could see clearly. Sunshine pouring through the window made her long to get up and go outside.

"Wendy, what is my name?" asked the doctor.

Wendy turned her head to look at the woman beside the bed. She was pretty, with gray eyes, straight blond hair cut about chin length, and pale skin. Under her white smock she wore a black skirt, white blouse and low-heeled shoes. There was a plastic badge on her jacket, and Wendy was sure her name was on that, but the doctor had her hand over it.

"Don't you know your own name?" Wendy asked. "Maybe you should be in this bed instead of me."

The doctor tried to hide her smile and kept looking at Wendy with serious gray eyes.

"Let's see, starts with a P. Paulette? No. Pearl? Parker? Patty? Oh, I've got it! Pamela. Dr. Pamela Morgan."

The doctor smiled for real this time. "I see your sassy bone isn't broken. That's good."

"Will you answer my questions?" asked Wendy, and the doctor nodded. "Where am I, and what have I done to myself? And when can I get out of here? I have things to do."

"You are in Marlett Medical Center, and from what I have heard from your parents and friends, you fell off an eight-foot wooden fence when you were trying to climb over it to rescue a dog. Then some man tried to jerk you up by your arm, which didn't help. You have three cracked ribs on your left side, and you broke your right leg. Your cast starts at the knee. Does it feel heavy?"

Wendy nodded and lifted the sheet up to peer at her leg. There was a bright white cast on her right leg from the knee down. Her toes were free, and she wiggled them.

"I'm afraid you're going to have to wear that for awhile."

"Can I ride a bicycle with this thing?"

"Some people can manage it, and I would bet you're able to. But you will have to be very careful for a few days about those ribs. You might want to avoid the bicycle for awhile. Your other injury was the one we worried about the most but I think you just showed me that you are OK. You conked your head pretty hard when you fell, and you have a concussion. It's a brain injury, what we call a sleepy brain. That's why you've been drifting in and out so much. It's also why you don't remember some things right before and right after the fall."

"Will I ever remember that stuff?"

"Most likely not. But your brain will be fine after awhile."

"How long? It's almost time for the *Bugle* to come out, and I have stories to write." With her right arm, she flipped back the covers and started to move her right leg. Pain shot all the way up her right side. She winced.

Dr. Morgan moved closer to the bed and patted Wendy's arm. "We'll get you out of that bed in a little while to walk. But you will have to have someone with you because you're very weak and you'd fall by yourself. And we can't have that."

"And can you call Wanda and Terry Wright and ask them to come get me?"

"Your parents have been here around the clock, and so have your friends, too many for the room sometimes. We didn't know when you'd wake up, I mean really wake up, so we sent them all home. The nurse is calling your parents now."

"When can I go home?"

"We'll see. Not today." Dr. Pamela paused, waiting for another question. But Wendy was silent.

"Is there anything else you want to ask me?"

Wendy shook her head. She didn't feel like talking any more. She was worried about how much school she would miss and wondered what Tina would do about the stories she was supposed to write for the next edition of the *Bugle*. She'd never be able to catch up and thinking about it made her tired. She closed her eyes, even though she left them open just enough to watch Dr. Morgan, who wrote something on her chart then moved around the room, opening the blinds, fluffing up the pillows behind Wendy's head, admiring the flowers on the shelf near her bed. Finally, she patted Wendy's hand and left. Wendy wondered what she'd written on the chart. Probably "Clumsy patient needs to stay an extra week."

She must have drifted off to sleep. The next thing she knew, she smelled her mother's perfume and someone was kissing her forehead. Her eyes flew open and there was Wanda. She had never been so glad to see her mother. She raised both arms for a hug, even though it hurt, and Wanda hugged her gingerly. "I don't want to break any more ribs," she said.

"How mad are you?"

Her mother smiled. "It's hard to be mad at someone in a

hospital bed."

Just then Wendy's dad came in. "I've just been talking to Dr. Morgan," he said to Wanda, then realized Wendy was awake. He wanted to hug her, but seemed afraid to. So he leaned over and pecked her on the cheek.

She wanted to know what Dr. Morgan told her father, but didn't get a chance to find out because Luella and Tina showed up, and with them came Libby and Riley. Soon the room was noisy with everyone gathered around Wendy's bed, and several conversations were going at once. Finally Wendy raised her hand, and everyone looked at her.

"Can anyone tell me how much longer I have to stay here?"

Her father looked guilty, and she knew that's what he and Dr. Morgan had been talking about. Wendy stared at him until he spoke.

"The doctor doesn't know. She wants to get you out of bed and walking first. She knows as soon as you go home, you're going to want to resume your regular activities."

This annoyed her. She turned to Riley. "How is Roomer?" she asked.

"Gaining weight. My father bakes him these special biscuits with a lot of suet in them, and Roomer eats about ten a day. That's in addition to his dog food."

A picture flashed into her head of a brown tasseled shoe kicking him. "Did he have broken ribs or anything like that?" she asked.

"We had him checked out by a vet in Marlett. Dad called him and told him what had happened, and he made a special trip to our house so Roomer wouldn't have to travel in a car. He felt his ribs and said none were broken. But they were bruised. Roomer whined when the doctor touched them. That and malnutrition were the only things wrong with him."

"What about the sores all over his legs and back?"

"Oh yeah, and that." Riley looked at Libby quickly, and didn't say anything.

"But what caused them?"

"Wendy, you don't need to know…" began her mother.

Wendy's eyes locked on Riley. "I know the vet must have had some theory," she said.

"Cigarettes. They were cigarette burns."

Wendy could feel her face getting hot, then her neck. She clenched her teeth so hard that her head began to hurt. She didn't say anything else, even when Luella asked if they could take her picture to go with the story they were writing about her.

Everyone grew silent, and no one would meet her eyes.

"I knew they were cigarette burns when I saw them," said Wendy, "and I know who put them there. I just wanted to make sure everyone else knew that, too."

Then the nurse who thought her name was Lucy came in and told everyone they would have to go, and Wendy knew they were relieved. They almost tripped over themselves telling her goodbye and hurrying out the door, all except for her parents and Libby, who got permission to stay awhile. Wendy was grateful, even though she couldn't show it.

—— Eighteen ——

Homecoming

If Dr. Morgan wanted me to leave in a wheelchair, why didn't she tell me that?" Wendy glared at the nurse's back, then at the chair she'd wheeled in. "She had me walking all over this place yesterday. So why do I have to be pushed out of here?"

"The doctor told me two things," said Mrs. Archie, who was putting Wendy's plants into a large box. "She said you would be cranky, and that you would have to ride in that chair. The doctor is never wrong."

"I don't want those plants," Wendy growled, only a little ashamed at how she sounded. "Just give 'em away."

"We have two patients down the hall with no family or friends here. They would love to have them. You don't want even one?"

Wendy shook her head. "I'll just take the cards. Why don't you take one home?"

"OK. This one." Mrs. Archie pointed to a bouquet of yellow irises and a spray of small white flowers. "And I'll make a deal with you. You let us push you in the wheelchair to the elevator, and sit in it until we get to the first floor. Then you can get up and walk the rest of the way."

"I don't want to be pushed at all!" whined Wendy. "I can walk!"

"That's the deal," said Mrs. Archie, shrugging. "Take it or leave it."

Having no choice, Wendy took it. She was mad about everything without knowing why, even though she had been thrilled earlier when Dr. Morgan came by and said she could go home. She hadn't even expected to see the doctor on Sunday morning, and had thought she'd have to spend another day in her tiny hospital bed, in the room with green-gray walls and chipped linoleum floors.

Dr. Morgan must have gotten tired of Wendy asking when she could leave. Or maybe she'd had Sunday in mind all along. She left instructions for the nurses to get Wendy out of bed to walk several times Saturday. The crutches would take some getting used to, but at least she knew she could do it.

Even the gray sky and Dr. Morgan's instructions that she was to stay home from school and the *Bugle* for a couple of days could not quench her desire to go home. She did not say Wendy had to lie in bed, and there was a lot you could do with a telephone and a legal pad. The solitude of the hospital had given Wendy lots of ideas for stories, and there was one in particular that needed to be done immediately.

When her parents arrived, Wendy glanced at Mrs. Archie and sat in the wheelchair without protest. She let herself be pushed to the elevator and sat in the chair all the way from the third to the first floor. She could sense Wanda's surprise at how docile she was.

The car stopped on the first floor. "You need to tell my parents about our deal, Mrs. Archie." said Wendy.

Terry Wright objected at the details. "I don't think that's a good idea. The wind is really strong," he said. "It could knock you down if you aren't careful."

Wendy looked at her mother, whom she'd expected to disagree first. Wanda just gazed at her, smiling slightly. She didn't say anything.

"Then give me my suitcase," she said to her father as Mrs. Archie rolled her wheelchair out of the elevator. "It will give me some added weight."

Her father shook his head. "If you're going to do it, both hands on the crutches," he said, pointing to the pair Wanda had tucked under her arm. Wendy eyed them. Her parents had rented them from the hospital medical supply. They didn't look too different from the ones she had used before.

She rose from the chair without help, though her mother looked as if she was ready to leap into action at any moment, and watched as Mrs. Archie adjusted the crutches. "Remember to keep the weight off that right leg," she said as Wendy secured the crutches under her arms.

She took a few steps away from them, careful to keep her right leg bent so that she wouldn't use it. Then she came back.

"How long do I have to use these?" she asked Mrs. Archie.

"As long as you have that cast on your leg. Remember, no weight on that right leg."

"Especially not my weight, right?"

Mrs. Archie looked at her as if she didn't understand. Wendy knew she was just being polite.

In the car heading home, the fatigue hit. She was troubled that it took so little to tire her out, but she could not fight it. Anyway, it wasn't like there was anything new to see, and the sky was so dreary she'd rather close her eyes. She dozed until they got home and then went to her bed to lie down just for a moment. When Wanda woke her up to say that she had a visitor, it was four in the afternoon.

"Is that clock right?" asked Wendy.

Wanda nodded.

"Then there must be something wrong with me. I can't be sleeping all the time like this."

"Here," said Wanda, handing her the crutches. "Go wash your face before you talk to Luella."

"Oh, no," groaned Wendy, even thought she was secretly pleased. "What does she want?"

"You'll have to come out and see," said Wanda, gliding away. "Be sure to comb your hair."

Luella had brought her camera again. She got up from her chair as Wendy thumped into the family room. Crutches did not let you enter a room quietly.

Wendy plopped down in a chair and put her right leg up on an ottoman.

"Are you going to let me take your picture today?" demanded Luella.

"Do I have a choice?"

Luella shook her head.

"What's the story about?"

"Your part in Roomer's rescue."

"It's not sappy, is it?"

"I'm writing it, so what do you think?" said Luella as she checked out everything on her camera.

"Do I get to read the story before it gets in the paper?"

"What do you think?" asked Luella again.

"But I work there!"

"All the more reason that you don't get to read it in advance. You'd go back and make your own changes. You know that violates everything I taught you."

Wendy sat quietly, pouting, while the editor snapped a

dozen photos from every possible angle. "These pictures would look better if you would attempt a smile," said the editor.

So Wendy did, losing her self-consciousness as Luella took picture after picture. She was finishing up when Wendy asked, "What did you do to help Burnam?" Luella put down the camera and got out her notepad. She wouldn't look at Wendy.

"I don't know what you mean."

Wendy sighed and rolled her eyes. "Someone who came to see me at the hospital said you took care of him. So what did you do?"

Luella flipped pages of the notebook until she got to the one she was looking for. "I need to ask you a couple of questions about your escapade, then I will be done," she said. She looked up at Wendy, who stared back, unblinking. "Riley and Carmen told me you were the one who called Libby to come and speak to the French maid. How did you know that Libby could speak French?"

"Geez, Luella," said Wendy, rolling her eyes, "we've been friends forever. I know everything about Libby! Why is that important?"

Luella looked at her sternly. "Didn't I ever tell you that there are no dumb questions?"

"Yes, but apparently you were mistaken!"

Luella glared but didn't respond. "What were you thinking when you looked over the fence and saw Roomer tied below?"

Wendy shrugged and widened her eyes. "There he is?"

"Are you going to cooperate or not?" demanded Luella.

"Not. Answer my question and I will answer yours."

"OK. I told Horton that if saw another mark on his son, or heard that he had touched him, I would expose him in the *Bugle*. He said he would sue me. I told him we understood each other."

Wendy stared at Luella's red face. The editor bellowed a

lot, but never threatened. What she had done went against everything she preached about not getting involved in a story and about not using your position as a newspaper person to threaten someone.

"How long do you think that will work?" asked Wendy.

Luella shook her head. "Not very long," she admitted.

"I'll answer your questions now, but then I have a story idea."

"I can't wait," said Luella sarcastically, going over her notes. She asked a few more questions, then started to put the notebook away. So Wendy hurriedly told her about the idea she'd gotten while in the hospital for a story that needed to be done right away, and Luella began shaking her head before Wendy even got a complete sentence out.

"No, no, no!" she said, looking at Wendy. "You want to drive me out of business? That's the kind of story you do if you're a really big newspaper with lots of people to back you up – attorneys and things. I am just a small-town editor, trying to make a living. I thought you wanted to save the *Bugle*. We do that story, and Horton will own it!"

"It doesn't have to be specifically about him, and a story on child abuse is not going to drive you out of business," said Wendy quietly. "It's going to get you more readers. People need to know about it and what to do about it."

Luella sat with her purse on her lap and her camera slung over her shoulder, ready to leave. Yet she didn't. She stared at the floor, thinking. "Why would we be doing it now? You can't just start a series about child abuse without tying it to something that happened recently."

"That's the problem, Luella. Child abuse happens every day, and it's covered up so there is no obvious news story until someone is hurt or dead. Adults who are doing it don't want anyone to know about it. You have to find your own news."

Luella was shaking her head.

"OK," said Wendy, "the news can be Roomer, how he was found abused, tied to a stake. We can detail his injuries and talk about people who abuse animals…"

"Now you are talking crazy! Any stories we do about Roomer will just say that he has been found. Horton wasn't charged with anything for keeping that dog tied to a stake, and even if he was, it wouldn't be a big enough crime for us to put it in the paper."

"He wasn't charged for starving him, or for burning him with cigarettes? Or kicking him? I bet you haven't even checked. Besides, it's a fact that he had the dog tied to a short rope in his yard. A bunch of people saw it, and he could not deny that. You could call him and ask him why he had the dog tied to the stake."

Luella started for the door. She was shaking her head. "I think that fall injured your head worse than we thought. You need more rest. I'm going to leave so you can get it."

Wendy saluted her from her lair. She didn't feel like getting up, and Luella obviously was going to let herself out. The door closed loudly, and in a moment Wanda came into the room.

"Luella's gone already? I was going to ask her if she wanted some coffee."

Wendy started to tell her mother why Luella had left so quickly, but the ringing doorbell interrupted her. Her mother went to the door and Wendy sat in her chair, wondering if Luella had come back to yell some more. From her perch, she could see only the open door and part of her mother's head, nodding. She could hear some of Wanda's words, but that was all. "Why don't you come in and tell her yourself?" she was asking.

The next thing Wendy knew, Burnam Horton walked into the den and her mother disappeared. He kept his head down and looked guilty, but he kept walking until he was right in front of Wendy.

"Hi," he said. "Are you OK now?"

"I guess so. I'm glad to be home."

"I don't know how much of anything you remember from the hospital." He looked at her hopefully, and she realized he had told her something there that he was hoping not to repeat. She shook her head.

"All I remember is you being there with Mrs. Martino. Thanks for coming."

"She made me." He was looking at the floor. "That didn't come out right. I really would have come without her making me, but…I know I'm not your friend. She told me it would be OK if I went with her."

He stopped, and Wendy thought he was waiting for her to say something. That he was her friend, maybe? She wasn't ready to say that. She had not forgotten his nickname for her.

"Anyway, I wanted you to know that I was working at the *Bugle* and why. You remember asking me what kind of grade I got on the essay we were supposed to write about whether the new business might hurt or help a small town? It was a D. I figured you knew that," he said as Wendy nodded slightly. "Anyway, Mrs. Martino told me I could make it up by doing something worthwhile, and suggested helping out at the *Bugle* with everybody else. I thought she was kidding, but she wasn't. Do you mind if I work there?"

"Not if you stay out of my way. And don't call me or my friends names anymore."

He shook his head. "No. I won't…I…I'm sorry about that."

She stared at him. This was not the Burnam Horton she

knew. But then she was not the Wendy Wright she had been, either. "I wasn't sure it was a D," she said. "I mean, nobody told me."

"I figured you knew I flunked. I should have, for what I wrote. By the way, thank you for what you did," he said.

She was stunned. "For what I did?"

He nodded. "You know. Saving the dog and all. I didn't…I couldn't…anyway…thanks. I think you are real brave."

She stared at his shirt. As usual, it was long-sleeved even though it was seventy-five degrees outside. It was buttoned up to the neck. Luella's threat had not worked for very long at all.

"Burnam…is everything OK? At your home, I mean."

"Uh-huh. I have to go now."

"You want a soda? Or some cookies? My mom will get you anything you want."

"No, I have to go," he said, a tone of insistence creeping into his voice. Then he looked at her. "See ya in school when you get back." Then he hurried to the door.

As Wendy wondered if she was going to get any more surprises, her mother came back.

"Your visitors don't stay long," she remarked. "Can I get you anything?"

She shook her head and then blurted out to Wanda what she'd asked Luella to do. "But she said no, that it would run her out of business."

Her mother didn't say anything as she straightened books and magazines in the room. "Can I get you anything to read?"

"Yesterday's *Bugle*?" Wendy asked hopefully, and her mother went to get it.

When Wanda returned with it, Wendy asked her, "Did you wonder why Burnam was wearing a long-sleeved shirt buttoned all the way to the neck?"

"I hadn't noticed, to tell you the truth. I'm going to go start supper now. Call if you need something."

Wendy was exasperated. No one would listen to her, and she had never been so certain that something needed to be done. She closed her eyes and leaned her head against the back of the chair. She didn't notice her mother staring at her thoughtfully before she silently left the room.

── Nineteen ──

Parent Brigade

During the time she was in the hospital, Wendy had missed one installment of "Cheeky and Claude," and she caught up on the story while she was at home. In recent strips, Claude had helped Cheeky find Lorena Caldwell's special potion, the one that helped "stop crime, end drought, make the sun shine and the flowers grow."

Cheeky followed the trail to the yard of Pursley Meanbone, the town evildoer, and Claude, though ill, had used his detective skills to sniff it out and dig it up. Pursley was powerless without the potion. He left town, and the citizens were so happy, they threw a party for Claude and Cheeky.

The big Pyrenees had not been flat on his side since. He had even gained weight.

In the most recent strip, Claude was still able to tie his trenchcoat, but was gaining girth. Cheeky warned him that he needed to cut back on the dog biscuits.

"You nag me when I don't eat, and nag me when I do," Claude muttered in the final panel. Wendy chuckled. Cheeky reminded her of Wanda sometimes.

She remembered the comic strip as she searched for clothes for school Tuesday morning. Her mother tapped on the door and opened it a crack. "OK if I come in?" She asked through the slit.

"Sure."

Wanda walked only a couple of steps into the room, then awkwardly thrust a bag at Wendy. "I got these for you in Marlett last week, thinking I'd give them to you for your birthday," she said. "But that's a month away, and today is a special day, too. You haven't been in school. So, here. I hope they fit."

Wendy took the bag just as awkwardly. Her mother almost never bought her clothes. She'd given up a long time ago trying to get Wendy to wear something besides sweats. When the occasion demanded it, Wendy would wear a shapeless dress or jumper, or nicer pants, but mostly she avoided events where she had to dress up.

She opened the bag slightly and looked in. She saw a flash of red, and her heart sank. Why would you buy a fat person red?

She put the bag on the bed and tried to smile. "Thanks, Mom."

"Aren't you going to look at what's in there? When I saw it, I immediately thought of your dark hair and eyes and knew it was for you. The skirt is just a basic gray, but will go with a lot of things. And gray and red look especially—"

"I can't wear red."

"Why not?"

"You know fat people can't wear red!" Wendy exploded.

Her mother took Wendy's arm. "Get your crutches and come with me. I need to show you something."

The crutches were leaning against her bed. Wendy grabbed them, muttering "I don't know why I can't just wear what I want," and followed her mother into her parents' bedroom. They went to a full-length mirror right beside her parent's walk-in closet. "Now," said Wanda, standing beside Wendy. "Put your crutches down and use my shoulder to lean on. I want you to look at yourself."

"I don't want to," whined Wendy.

"I don't think you ever look at yourself," insisted her mother. "Open your robe and look."

"Will you leave me alone if I do?"

Wanda nodded, so Wendy did as she asked, hastily untying her robe, looking at herself, and then covering herself up again.

"You didn't really look," Wanda chastised her, handing Wendy the crutches.

"There's something weird about standing in front of a mirror with your mother wearing only your underwear. It's embarrassing."

"I'm sorry. I didn't mean to embarrass you. Listen, wear whatever you want to school, but keep those clothes for a few days, all right? I can return them if you don't want them, and we'll get something you do want. I have something to do this morning, so I didn't fix breakfast. I put cereal and other stuff out for you. And I've arranged for Mr. Davis to pick you up. In a few days you can see about riding your bike, but not yet."

She kissed Wendy on her forehead and left her standing in the middle of the master bedroom. Wendy headed back to her own room, secretly pleased at what she'd seen in the mirror. Still, she wanted to wear her sweats to school. She told herself she was lucky to find something that would fit over her cast, and put the bag with the gray skirt and red top on the shelf.

She was waiting on the front porch when Riley and his dad pulled up in Mr. Davis's fifteen-year-old beige Buick wagon. The Davises also had a pickup truck and a new Ford sedan, but Mr. Davis always drove the Buick because he could get almost anything in it.

The sun glinted off Riley's spiky red hair as he jumped out of the car to grab Wendy's backpack and open the back door for her. "What manners!" said Wendy. "You've never…"

Suddenly she was greeted by a pink tongue the size of a beach towel as Roomer bounded across the back seat and licked her face. Knocked off balance, she almost fell backward, but Riley, standing behind her, grabbed her shoulders. She leaned on her crutches as she scratched the dog's ears and neck and said silly words to him. His ribs still showed and his hair was matted down around the neck where the rope had been, but he had gained weight and obviously felt better, just like Claude. The sores on his legs were healing.

As she heaved herself into the back seat, making room for her injured leg, Roomer backed up, getting out of her way. Then he rested beside her on his belly, his big paws hanging off the back seat and his tail thumping.

"He looks good, Mr. Davis," she said as Riley shut the door. "He lets you put medicine on his sores without trying to snap at you?"

"Roomer and I understand each other," came the reply. "He'd do almost anything for my homemade doggie gourmet dinners and the treats I bake for him. I found recipes in an old book I bought at the library book sale. In another couple of weeks, as soon as he puts on a little more weight, he can go back to school. But I think you and Riley and the others, maybe some of the teachers, should figure out a rotation system for him to go home with someone on weekends and holidays and in the summers."

"Don't you want to keep him, Mr. Davis?" Roomer's tail again began thumping against the back of the seat at the sound of Wendy's voice, and he nudged her arm with his nose so she would pet him.

Mr. Davis shook his head. "The school is his home, Wendy, and the students and teachers are his pack. He stayed there because he knew he belonged. He's already anxious to get back."

Wendy was anxious to get back, too, although she would not have admitted it. She hadn't even missed a full week, but it felt like a month. She missed Libby and Riley and her classes.

Libby was waiting for them at the front of the school. "Look what she's wearing!" Wendy whispered to Riley. Libby wore jeans, boots, and a dove gray sweater set that would have been at home at a dress-up tea. Around her neck was a string of pearls that matched the sweater. On Libby it all looked right.

"She's been dressing like that all the time," said Riley. "You know, sort of how she dressed the day you fell off the fence. I forgot to tell you."

"My mom and I agreed to compromise," Libby said as she saw Wendy staring at her outfit. "The jeans and boots are my choice, and the sweater set, hers. What do you think?"

Wendy walked all around her, nodding. "It's you," she said. "I don't know anyone else who could pull it off. It's….it's…Moffatt Corner French."

The three of them talked and griped and waited for the first bell. It was as if Libby had never been angry with her. They were together as much as possible throughout the day, just like old times.

By the end of the day, though, Wendy was exhausted from telling her story over and over and from maneuvering around the corridors with her backpack and crutches. Riley and Libby carried her pack when they were there, but that wasn't always possible.

Wendy was glad to see Mr. Davis's station wagon parked outside the school, Roomer's head poking out the window. Wendy hadn't realized how many kids knew Roomer until she heard them pointing and yelling his name. Many ran to the car to pat his head.

"*Bugle* taxi!" cried Mr. Davis as Wendy and Riley got into the car. "Doesn't anyone else want to ride with us?"

Libby and Carmen piled in beside Wendy and Roomer. Then Wendy saw Burnam coming down the sidewalk and motioned him toward the car. He shook his head and shoved his hands deeper into his pockets as he walked by.

"Why would you want him to ride with us?" Libby demanded.

Carmen didn't say anything, but her dark eyes fixed on Wendy as she waited for the answer. From his position in the front seat, Riley twisted around. The question was on his face, too.

"Because he needs a friend. And anyway, he's not so bad. Did you know he came to see me in the hospital?"

No one answered, but Mr. Davis looked at her in the rearview mirror and smiled. She thought he nodded his head a bit, too. She knew her friends didn't really understand, but nobody said anything else about it. They all knew what Burnam's father did to him.

Roomer got out with them at the *Bugle* office, and Mr. Davis drove off. Wendy was glad, but she wondered if the dog was well enough to walk all the way home.

160

"Here they are, Luella!" Tina called when they all walked in.

It took a few moments for Luella to emerge from her office, and she was red-faced. "Are you OK?" Wendy asked.

"Yes, why do you ask?"

Wendy shrugged. "You look like you do when you're arguing with someone on the phone," she said.

Luella didn't respond, but picked up her camera from Tina's desk and looked around the office, stroking her chin. Finally she pointed toward a blank wall. "OK," she said, "you four go over there, and kneel. Except we'll put Wendy in a chair. Make sure Roomer sits next to her."

"What's this all about?" Wendy asked.

"I wasn't happy with those pictures I took of you. I realized that Roomer was missing. And the rest of the rescue team. So I need to get some more photos, and no whining!"

Wendy pretended to be out of sorts, but she was glad that Luella had thought of this. She wasn't the only one who'd rescued the dog. She was just the only one stupid enough to fall off the fence.

"I want to be on the floor with everyone else," she told Tina, who'd found a chair for her.

"OK. But do you think you can kneel?"

Wendy nodded. With Libby steadying her by holding onto one arm, she got down on her uninjured leg first, then the one with the cast. The others settled around her. Roomer stood by Luella, watching. When they called him, he came running, and the first picture snapped was Roomer's big pink tongue licking Wendy's face. Luella took at least ten more with Roomer sitting in the middle of them.

"OK, that'll do," she told them. "Tina will get you started on your assignments. I have a meeting to finish up."

"Who is she meeting with?" Wendy asked Tina as Luella hurried down the corridor and shut the door.

Tina didn't answer but looked toward the door as Burnam came in. "Wendy, I'd like for you to help Burnam with his story today. The rest of you need to finish up everything in the next hour. The press starts at six-fifteen, and we start paying overtime after eight. So step on it."

Wendy frowned at Tina for ignoring her question, but turned to Burnam. "We'll work over there," she said, pointing to a desk away from the action.

She discovered that Burnam wrote his stories in a notebook, then transferred that to the computer, the way a lot of beginners worked. Thus he had two notebooks, one with all his notes on a story about a new karate studio in Marlett, and one with several pages of the story itself. Wendy was impressed when she read it.

"This is good, Burnam." She glanced at him. He was looking outside, and he shrugged at her words. "You just need to put in some quotes. See? Here and here. You have them in your notes, I think." She pointed out a couple of places in his notes that he had quotes, and he nodded. "You also have all the ages of the students, but it's not in your story. Here's how you do it," she said, showing him how to insert the ages so that the story still flowed.

Burnam was looking at her now, instead of outside. "And then, all this information about class times and prices, and the phone number to call, can go at the end of your story. That way, you answer those questions for people, but the answers don't get in the way of you telling the story."

"How do you know all this?" he asked.

"Years of reading a paper, and then the time I've spent up here. There's a computer no one is using. You can transfer everything to it and insert the other stuff. And from now on, you should write all your stories on the computer. You're doing double work by writing them in a notebook first."

"My typing's no good," he said. "Can't someone else type it in?"

"We don't have time for that, Burnam. Everyone has to pull his own weight. You know how to type, right?"

He nodded. "I'm just slow."

"You'll get faster if you do it every day." Wendy set him up on the computer and watched as he began his story. Soon he was immersed in the work, and she headed back toward Tina's desk to find out once and for all who was in Luella's office.

Just then, the door to the office opened and people started walking out, Luella leading the way. She pointed them toward the back door instead of the front area, where the students were working. No one saw Wendy, who was standing in the hall-way, watching as the Davises came out, then Mrs. Weaver, then Mr. Degarcia, then a woman in a suit that Wendy didn't know. She guessed that her parents would be next, and she was right.

Wendy looked around the room. Everyone was working, and no one had seen them but her. She headed toward her back-pack on Tina's desk, and pulled out a sheaf of papers. "Don't you have a story due?" asked Tina, without looking up.

"Yes. It's almost finished. I'm just waiting for a computer. But right now I need to show Luella something."

"Now's not good. She's in a meeting," said Tina, who was editing a story and still didn't look up.

"They all just left," said Wendy.

Then Tina looked at her.

"I know why they were here," said Wendy. "Except I can't figure out who the woman I the suit is."

"She's a lawyer from Marlett. Your parents brought her."

"A lawyer! So they're suing Luella for hiring us? Why can't they just ask her to stop using us as reporters?"

Tina looked startled. "No one is suing anyone, Wendy. Just go talk to Luella before everyone else hears us! This is not a subject we should be discussing here." She was looking at Burnam's back.

Clutching the sheaf of papers to her chest, Wendy knocked on Luella's closed door and went in without waiting for a response. The editor was sucking on a piece of hard candy from a dish on her desk. "I'm trying to quit smoking, so enter at your own risk. I guess you wonder who all those people were. I saw you watching them."

"I know who all of them were except for the lawyer."

"Then you know why they were here."

Wendy had learned from Luella the art of looking at someone without speaking to get more information, which is what she did now.

"They convinced me that the *Bugle* should do the series on child abuse. All the parents told me how important it was and said they would support the *Bugle* in any way possible. They even found the lawyer to be my legal adviser. For a reduced fee that I can pay in installments."

She and Wendy stared at each other for a moment. "I see where you get your determination and stubbornness," Luella added. "Your mother set up the whole meeting this morning. I told her when she called that I didn't have time but she promised it wouldn't take long and kept at it until I agreed. The series will start in a couple of weeks. Your mother is going to help edit it. Part One is going to be about what happens to adults to make them child abusers. Roomer is going to be a part of that story. I will write it myself."

Wendy still stared, but this time because she was speechless.

"Well, what's the matter?" Luella asked crossly.

"My mother set up the meeting? Wanda Wright? And that same person is going to help with the editing?"

"Right. She called me Monday morning and said it was important to you, so it was important to her. I asked her to help edit when she told me she was an English major. I figure both you and your sister must have come by your talents naturally."

"I never thought of that."

"Let that be a lesson to you. Even people you think you know can surprise you. Now go on and let me do some work."

"Wait," said Wendy, holding out a thick stack of papers she had carried into Luella's office. "You'll need this. It's research I did at the library on child abuse Monday."

"When you were supposed to be resting at home?"

"The doctor didn't say anything about the library," said Wendy, getting up. "I have a story to finish, so I'll be going. What's the rest of the series?"

"I haven't gotten that far yet, but I expect you and your friends will all be writing some of it."

"What about Burnam?"

"I don't know," said Luella. "I haven't gotten that far, either."

—— Twenty ——

Roomer Rescues Bugle

Luella made a special deal with the president of the Parent-Teacher Association of Riddle Middle School so that every student got a copy of the next day's *Bugle*. Wendy rought hers from home, just in case there were not enough to go round.

"Where are you taking that?" Wanda asked her as she tucked it nto her book bag.

"To school."

"You be sure to bring it home. I want to keep it."

Wendy tried to hide her smile.

"It doesn't mean I'm going to start reading the *Bugle* every day," Wanda added. "But if there's a story about you in it, I want to keep t."

"OK," said Wendy.

"I should probably keep them anyway if you're going to keep writing stories for it," added Wanda.

"Right," said Wendy.

The night before she had thanked her mother for talking to Luella about the child abuse series, and for organizing the parents of her friends to talk to the editor. And for finding Luella an attorney. Wanda had blushed and said, "I'm just doing my job." She had smiled when Wendy asked her who wrote the job description for mothers, and then hastily changed the subject.

"Are you ready to go?" Wanda asked Wendy. "You still want to do this?"

Wendy nodded. She and her mother had agreed she could ride her bicycle to school if she rode slowly. She had practiced riding around the block last night. It was awkward with the cast, but once she got astride the bike and got going, she could do it.

Her mother watched her get on the bike and pedal slowly down the driveway, then waved and went back inside. Wendy knew she would call the school in a little while to be sure she made it.

She was a bit later getting to school that morning, and everyone was already studying the newspaper when she walked into Mrs. Martino's class. The teacher smiled and handed her a newspaper as she sat down, not mentioning her tardiness.

"I'm sorry to be late. I rode my bike, and it was slow going."

"It's all right. Riley and Libby told me. We're reading the *Bugle*."

Wendy sat down and looked at the *Bugle* again, even though she had the story memorized. At the top of page one, under a huge headline that read "Roomer's Rescue" was the main photo, a picture of Roomer and Wendy, the dog's broad pink tongue swiping Wendy's nose. Libby, Carmen and Riley were gathered behind them. All of them were grinning, even the dog.

Below that was a smaller photo of Wendy at home, half of her in shadow, her cast-covered leg elevated on an ottoman. She was gazing out the window. Even Wendy liked the shot. It looked the way she'd felt, pensive and a bit adrift, on her first day home from the hospital. She couldn't remember Luella taking the picture.

The story, with four bylines, started to the right of the pictures. Luella had asked Wendy to write it as it happened to her instead of making it a news story, but Wendy had said that wouldn't work.

"It's not about me. It's about the rescue of Roomer, and a bunch of people played a part. When the story tells about me falling off the fence and going to the hospital, someone else has to take over because I can't remember that part."

"But I don't want four bylines!" Luella had complained.

"That's how many people covered the story," said Wendy shrugging. She would not budge. And as Luella read the final draft last evening, Wendy could tell she was pleased.

So was Wendy, as she listened to Mrs. Martino reading the story out loud. The room was hushed except for her voice. Anyone who had the bad luck to sniff too loud or clear his throat got a glare from everyone else.

Mrs. Martino read, in her clear, schoolteacher voice:

"Riddle Middle School's longtime mascot, a chocolate Labrador mix named Roomer, was rescued last week by four students from a back yard where he'd been tied up on a 2-foot rope and tortured. He had not been seen for at least 10 days.

"One of the dog's rescuers, Wendy Wright, tumbled from the top of an 8-foot privacy fence during the mission, breaking her right leg and cracking three ribs. She also suffered a concussion when her head struck the ground and was unconscious for several minutes.

"Wendy, 14, returned to school Tuesday after an overnight stay in Marlett Medical Center and one day recuperating at home.

"Roomer, whose injuries included abrasions, cigarette burns and starvation, is recovering at the home of student Riley Davis, 15, another of his rescuers. Dr. Peter Brenner, a veterinarian from Marlett who traveled to Moffatt Corner to treat the dog because Moffatt Corner has no veterinarian, said Roomer will make a full recovery.

"No charges have been filed against the homeowner who tied up the dog.

"Roomer had not been seen at the school since April 7, when he ran off with a hat blown off the head of an audience member at the Easter fashion show at Riddle High School Auditorium. He was discovered tied in a back yard on Weeping Willow Lane after the *Bugle* received an anonymous tip on his whereabouts."

As Mrs. Martino continued reading, Wendy thought about the argument she'd had with Luella over identifying Mr. Horton as the owner of the house. Naming the street was the closest Luella had let them come to telling where Roomer was kept prisoner. She had told them they could not give the specific address nor identify anyone, since no one had been charged with a crime.

"But why hasn't he?" Wendy had asked her.

"That's not our concern right now. Concentrate on reporting the facts as you know them and can support them," said Luella. "You don't know that he is the person who tied up or abused the dog."

"But we can support that Roomer was tied at 4030 Weeping Willow. We all saw him there. The ambulance came there to get me! It should be in their records!

"And if Mr. Horton says otherwise?"

"He'd be lying!"

"And it would be your word against his," said Luella. "But if he is charged, then the accusation is supported by a police record, and I will approve putting his name, address and other details in the paper."

"It's more than an accusation, Luella. It's a fact. And Mr. Horton will probably never be charged with anything."

"In our country, a person is innocent until proven guilty in a court of law. So Wendy Wright and her friends cannot proclaim Mr. Horton guilty and demand punishment. It has to go through our legal process first. A record at the police station is the first step."

"So it's our word against the police department's, and you believe them," said Wendy.

"That is an oversimplification," said Luella, "but yes. I have to protect the Bugle, and this is the only way I know how to do it."

Wendy pushed the conversation out of her head by counting the gasps she heard from her classmates as they heard the story. By the time Mrs. Martino finished reading, she had counted four loud ones at the words "torture," "tumbled," "cigarette burns" and "no charges." She didn't count the less noticeable puffing sounds. But she noted that the story held everyone's attention. Even the kids who always appeared bored were sitting up straight and following every word Mrs.Martino spoke.

Then Wendy glanced at Burnam and wished she hadn't. His army of friends had disappeared. He was sitting by himself in a back corner. He was stooped over his desk, eyes down, his right index finger tracing an invisible pattern round and round. She turned away before he saw her looking at him and tried not to think about what he must be feeling.

As soon as Mrs. Martino finished reading the story, hands went up. Everyone had a question, and the first one, from Katy Carver, concerned the lack of identification. "Whose house was it?" she asked Mrs. Martino. "Why wasn't there an arrest? Isn't it a crime to torture a dog?"

"Let's ask our reporters," said Mrs. Martino. "All of them are your classmates, as you know. Wendy, can you tell us why the person who held Roomer captive is not named in the story?"

A deep breath and the awareness of Burnam sitting by himself in the back of the room helped Wendy get her bearings. All eyes were on her as she spoke. "I'm sure everyone is familiar with the concept 'innocent until proven guilty'," she said, glancing around the room. Heads nodded.

"We couldn't report whose house it was unless the police department decided to file charges, and they haven't. They are still investigating. We could accuse someone unfairly if we print a name without any police action to back it up. And even that doesn't mean that anyone charged with a crime actually did it. But if police file charges, then it's a public record, at least in this state, and that's when you can report it."

"But you know where the house is. So can you tell us who it is?" asked Katy.

"Yeah! Tell us!" chimed in other voices. "Let's go over to the house and TP it!" cried another.

"Or spray-paint it!" exclaimed a voice on the other side of the room.

Wendy looked around at the familiar freckled faces she saw almost every day of her life. In their eyes she saw anger and vengeance. It made her afraid. She could tell that even Libby, Riley and Carmen wanted her to say whose house it was. She glanced again at the back of the room again and saw Burnam sitting perfectly still now in his long-sleeved blue shirt, his hands folded in his lap. He didn't even appear to be breathing.

"We can't do that," said Wendy, quietly but firmly. "We would be as bad as the person who tortured Roomer."

"But what if the police don't do anything?" cried Katy.

"They won't!" exclaimed someone else. "That's the rich part of town. They can do anything they want over there! It's not fair!"

As other students chimed in, Wendy shot a pleading look at Mrs. Martino. The teacher was silent as she stood at the front of the class, but she stared in turn at each person who spoke. One by one, they fell silent.

"This has been a good exercise in democracy," she said. "You've all gotten to express your opinion. But let me ask you something…how would you feel if this happened at your house, and there had been no charges filed, and it appeared in the paper anyway?"

"Bad," said Herman Stuver. "But I'd feel bad if charges were filed, too."

"It would never happen, Herman," said someone at the back. "Everyone knows you're afraid of dogs!"

The class erupted in laughter. Mrs. Martino held up one hand and the room grew silent again. "OK," she said, "we're getting there slowly, but at least we are getting there. In this country, rights clash with each other. Our press is free, but with that freedom, it has to exercise responsibility. And one of the ways Ms. Cathcart does that is by refusing to print the names of people who might have committed a crime until it has reached the public record stage. She gives the police a chance to do their jobs first. That might not sound like a good thing to you in all situations, but consider how you might feel if the dog were tied up in your yard, but you didn't have anything to do with him being there. And then, all of a sudden, your name and address appear in the paper."

"The police could get it wrong, too," said Carmen. "And what if they do, and it gets in the paper anyway?"

Mrs. Martino nodded. "I am sure that situation has happened too, Carmen. But I think the newspaper would correct it if they got it wrong."

"How would a correction help the accused person?" asked Katy. "The newspaper should be sure it gets everything right the first time or not print it!"

Mrs. Martino looked at Wendy and smiled. Katy Carver and probably others had come full circle. "I think that's what the *Bugle* is trying to do, Katy," said Mrs. Martino. "Certainly it's not perfect and it makes mistakes. But I am sure it wants to make as few as possible."

Wendy could not go anywhere that day without attracting a crowd. The whole school had gotten copies of the *Bugle*, so everyone knew the story. Elementary school students wanted to sign her cast and carry her backpack. Middle school students who didn't work at the *Bugle* wanted to know how to sign up. Journalism students who worked on the high school newspaper interviewed her for a special edition of the Riddle High School *Roundup*. And everyone wanted to know when Roomer was coming back to school.

The Spirit Crew, a group of high school students charged with increasing school spirit, enlisted the high school cheerleaders to create a banner. It was presented to the principal in an impromptu ceremony Friday morning, and he drafted two custodians to go up on the roof and fasten it right below the name of the school. Under the words Riddle Middle School was the phrase, "Home of Heroes and Roomer, the Dog."

That led to so much attention that the five-day-a week newspaper in Marlett, the *Muse*, published its own story Sunday and got permission to use the *Bugle's* photos. Wendy, Riley, Carmen and Libby gave them an interview at the *Bugle* office Friday afternoon after getting permission from Luella.

The *Muse's* story wasn't nearly as good as the *Bugle's*; Luella said they should have asked permission to use that, too, in addition to the photos.

The next Tuesday, a news crew from the national television program "The Rest of the Story," called Luella to ask her about the kids who rescued the dog from its unnamed captor. Tina, who eavesdropped on the conversation, said later that Luella was actually nice to them and told them to come anytime and feel free to use her newspaper as its headquarters. "She also promised to make you kids available for interviews," Tina told the regulars, Wendy, Libby, Riley and Carmen. "So get ready."

"Does that mean we have to do it?" asked Wendy. "What if I have other plans when they arrive?"

"Don't you want to?" Libby asked her. "It's our chance to be on television! When would we ever get that chance again?"

Wendy shrugged. "Guess it'd be OK," she said, thinking about how television added ten pounds to your weight.

When Brigette Weaver heard about national television coming to town, she decided to take advantage of the attention by organizing a fund-raiser for a Moffatt Corner animal shelter built around the theme, "A Day for the Animals." Libby's mother had always rescued orphan animals, fed them and found homes for them, but she had never organized anything for them. These days, though, she wasn't so focused on Libby and was more into civic causes.

The school board granted permission for the fund-raiser to be on the front lawn of Riddle Middle School because it involved so many students. It expanded to the auditorium of the high school when plans included a book fair, a craft sale, and a bake sale in addition to a dunking booth, face-painting, story-telling, music and food vendors.

Meanwhile, Luella had several staff meetings with her *Bugle* regulars to tell them about the child abuse series and make assignments for it.

"This is related to Roomer's rescue, isn't it?" Carmen asked.

"Yes. We think there is more to the story than dog abuse," answered Luella.

"So you think Mr. Horton is abusing Burnam?" asked Libby.

"What we will try to do is uncover the facts that are supported by records," said Luella. "So far there are no records that Mr. Horton abuses anyone."

The silence that followed was tense. Everyone was in Luella's office, and she had been ready to pass out papers with assignments on them. She put them down on her desk, crossed her arms and looked at the semicircle of reporters.

"Exactly what do you want to accomplish by telling people that Mr. Horton is a child-abuser?" Luella asked.

No one answered for a moment. Then Wendy said, "I can't speak for the rest of us, but I want him to stop hitting Burnam. I want him to be arrested, if that's what it takes. Now he thinks he can do anything he wants and everyone will look the other way."

"And how would our printing that change anything, if there are no records to support he is hitting Burnam? Do you think us printing something in the paper could force the police to act if they feel they don't have enough evidence?"

"Maybe if a bunch of people called the police, then they would have to do something."

Luella tried to hide a rare smile. "I think you ought to trust me on this," she said softly. "What we are going to do may not be exactly what you want to happen, but it may have the same results. I promise we aren't going to just let everything drop. OK?"

Wendy nodded reluctantly, and Luella picked up her papers again. She said that Part One, the first story, would examine statistics from Moffatt Corner and Haymer County, which included both Moffatt Corner and Marlett. Luella had also found a doctor at the emergency room in Marlett who had agreed to be interviewed. Another story, if they could get it, would be an interview with a victim of child abuse. The subject of Part Two was how often child abusers got caught in Moffatt Corner, and what happened to them. The final story, Part Three, would cover programs to help the abuser and abused.

Luella would write the series and do many of the interviews. Libby and Riley volunteered to get the statistics, and Tina was interviewing the doctor.

"Wendy, I want you to work on the interview with the victim. Or victims," said Luella, glancing Wendy's way.

"How do I find them?"

Luella stared at her as if trying to communicate without speaking. "You'll figure out something," she said, finally. "Carmen, you will get statistics for Part Two and the programs for Part Three.

"This starts next week," continued Luella. "All stories for the series are due on Monday instead of Tuesday, so I will have time to solve any problems before we go to press."

"What kind of problems?" asked Wendy.

"I'm sure we can't even imagine them all," Luella said.

—— Twenty-One ——

A Hard Interview

The *Bugle* was spread out on the kitchen table, but Wendy wasn't reading it. She was staring at a scrap of blue paper with a phone number on it.

She had done this for two days, carrying the scrap of paper around in her pocket, afraid to dial the number. The tiny scrap had kept her awake two nights and preoccupied her at school. She had to do something about it.

Wanda floated into the room, humming, and Wendy hastily stuck the scrap back in her pocket.

"How about some toast and fruit for breakfast?" asked Wanda.

"OK."

"How long are you going to stare at that number?"

"What number?"

"The one you just put in your pocket." Even as Wanda bustled about, getting out the bread board, the bread knife, an orange from the refrigerator, a banana from the hook, she hadn't missed a thing. She turned to Wendy and held up the banana and the orange.

Wendy pointed to the orange, and her mother tossed it to her.

"Whose number is it?" Wanda asked.

"Burnam's," muttered Wendy.

"How'd you get it? I thought the number was unlisted."

"Luella had it. I got it from her Rolodex. It was just out there on Tina's desk," Wendy said a bit defensively.

"Why do you have it?"

Wendy paused. Should she tell her? Would her mother be horrified? Would she tell her not to do it? Wendy plunged ahead, deciding in a split second that honesty with her mother was best. Wanda always figured out everything anyway.

"I need to interview Burnam for the child abuse series, and I don't know how to ask him." She looked at her mother again. This time Wanda was frowning. Wendy steeled herself. Her mother hadn't said anything about the *Bugle* in a long time. No "Why do you work there?" or "I wish you would stop hanging around that place." Now it was all going to gush out.

But all she said was, "Why do you need to call his house?" said Wanda. "Why don't you talk to him at school?"

"Huh?"

"You wouldn't have to interview him at school. You could do it later, at the *Bugle* office. There are private places you could talk. But I think you should make the initial contact in person, in a place familiar to both of you. If you call his house, you run the risk of getting his father or someone else who doesn't want you to talk to him. It should be his decision, not someone else's."

This made so much sense that Wendy didn't know why she hadn't thought of it. She stole a look at her mother, who was buttering the toast. "What would you say to him?" she asked.

Wanda frowned again. "That's a harder one. He's going to be skittish. I think I'd say something like, 'Are you going to the

ing for the classroom.

Wendy could have kicked herself. She had jumped in too quickly. They had hardly ever exchanged whole sentences except to fight with each other. Just blurting out what she wanted was not the right thing to do. She should have given him a note.

She wondered whether to wait for Libby and Riley or go inside. They'd probably be here any minute, as more and more parents were dropping off their kids. But then the rain started to come down horizontally, and her slicker was already folded up. She was going to get drenched if she stood there any longer.

The girls' restroom was on her way, so she stopped in for some paper towels to dry off her shoe as best she could. She got a huge wad of them, trying to hold them, her slicker and her notebooks under one arm while using her crutches. As she walked into the classroom, an arm reached out and touched her own. She jumped, fear pushing her heart into her throat. Everything fell to the floor with a clatter.

Then Burnam was picking it all up. "I'm sorry. I didn't mean to make you drop everything," he mumbled, as he tried to scoop up her notebooks and slicker. He finally stood up and thrust it awkwardly at her. "Could we talk today?" he asked, staring at her stuff instead of looking at her. "I'd just like to get it over with."

"Um, sure...but you don't have to do it at all. If it's something you don't feel..."

"I want to. Today."

Students were entering the room in groups of two and three. He turned and walked to the back corner of the room. Hearing the jolly laughter and happy voices as she watched Burnam seek his hiding place made her realize how different their worlds were. Most of the kids managed to enter the common world of school once they got there. But she didn't think that was so for Burnam.

Wendy thought all day about what she would ask him, and when she had spare minutes, she'd carefully record each question on her lined reporter's notebook, leaving spaces for his answers. Burnam arrived at the *Bugle* that afternoon about the time he usually did, and they found a desk near the corridor that led to Luella's office, out of earshot of everyone. The office was so busy, no one even noticed them.

Wendy pulled out her notebook and looked at her questions, all lined neatly up with a precise amount of room, three lines, left between each question. It looked silly to her now. But how to begin? She glanced at Burnam, who was rolling up his sleeves.

He rolled up the left one first, in precise folds, to the elbow. Then the right one. Then he laid his arms on the table, palms up, so she could see his forearms. Time seemed to stop for a moment. Wendy devoted all the energy she could muster to not gagging. Her lips twitched; she kicked her left heel with her right foot and focused on the pain.

She inhaled deeply and let her breath out slowly, and finally she studied what he was showing her. She stared at the old and new discolorations from bruises, the cigarette burns, several welts. There was one awful sore, now healing, of unknown origin.

"You're doing good. The only other person who ever saw this stuff was a friend of my mother's who used to be a nurse. Mom took me to her because she knew she wouldn't tell. But she had to leave and go to the bathroom. I knew she was throwing up. A nurse." He shook his head.

"Does anyone else know? Anyone who can help you?" asked Wendy.

"I think everyone knows, sort of. You know, don't you? You must have — you wanted to talk about it. But just because everyone knows doesn't mean they can help. Because they don't really know and they don't want to accuse without proof. See, he's smart. You can see what he does to a dog and rescue the dog, but you can only guess he's doing it to his family, too. So you can't do anything about that."

"He does this to your mother, too?" asks Wendy.

Burnam nodded. "He started with her. She was from a poor family, though, and didn't have anywhere to go. He never gave her much money, but at least she had a house to live in. Then I was born. She tells me now that she didn't think he'd ever beat me or she'd have left before. I don't know why she thought that."

He stopped for a minute and looked off into the distance, except there wasn't anything to see. Wendy waited silently.

"He started on me when I was three. He used to whip me with a belt. He didn't start this other stuff until I got older. I was five or six then. My mother tried to stop him, but he'd give it to her even worse. One time he broke her arm and told her exactly what to say to the doctor who set it. She always goes to the same doctor. He's been my dad's doctor forever and he won't say anything."

"Why does she stay with him?"

Burnam shrugged. "I think she's so used to it that she thinks that's the way it's supposed to be. And it's still the money. She doesn't think she could make a living, I guess. It's not something we talk about. We don't talk about anything."

"I guess people wonder about that. If you or your mother did talk about it, told someone, I mean...well, that would be proof. Wouldn't it?"

"You have to wonder. Everyone treats him differently because he's got money and the Horton name. I don't know if anyone would listen. They saw what he did to the dog, and they didn't do anything about that. Anyway, I can't tell someone unless she does. She's my mother."

"Maybe she's waiting for you to make the first move," suggested Wendy.

Burnam tilted his head as he thought about this, as if it had never occurred to him. Then he shrugged again. Wendy had taken very few notes as they talked, but she felt as if everything he said was branded on her brain. She didn't think she'd ever forget it.

He talked some more, giving her details about some of the things his father had done, things she could not have imagined. He talked in a monotone, his sentences brief, and it was almost as if he were telling stories about horrors he'd seen inflicted on someone else.

Wendy just listened, not speaking much, writing words now and then.

"Are you using my name?" he asked suddenly.

"No," said Wendy.

"Everyone will know who it is anyway, I guess," he said. "They already know."

"Burnam, it isn't your fault. They know that, too."

Once again, he looked as if he had never thought of it that way.

"What will your father do when he reads it?" Wendy asked. "Maybe you and you mother shouldn't be there."

"He never reads the *Bugle*. Someone would have to point it out to him. Who'd be crazy enough to do that? Everyone is scared of him."

"I'm not," Wendy started to say, but caught herself. "You don't seem scared of him," she said instead.

"I don't seem scared now. But I am a lot. Mostly I'm scared for my mother. There were times she told me she had a plan for getting out. But she never says that any more. I think she has given up."

Wendy didn't talk much when she got home, and neither of her parents tried to coax her to speak. But Wanda came to her room after supper. "Did you do your interview today?"

Wendy nodded.

"I thought so. You need to talk?"

Wendy sighed. "It's too ugly to talk about. I'd rather just write it."

"OK. But I am here if you need to talk."

Wendy slept fitfully between awful nightmares about the stories Burnam had told her. The next morning, she wished she could go to the *Bugle* right away and write the story to get it out of her head. That made her feel guilty; the nightmares she wanted to get rid of were Burnam's life.

Twenty-Two

Where's Burnam?

Burnam was wrong about one thing; his father did read the *Bugle*. He reacted immediately to the first part of the series, which detailed the causes of child abuse, how it often started with spouses and then moved on to children in the family. The story gave detailed information about why abusers abused, and what they were likely to do if no one intervened. It told some of the heinous, real-life results of child abuse, including details that Wendy had given Luella.

There were three stories in the Wednesday *Bugle,* and Wendy had read each of them in advance. She beamed about the work they had done, and couldn't wait for the other stories to appear.

Her mother was engrossed in them when Wendy came into the kitchen that morning. "Hi, Honey," Wanda said, barely looking up. Wendy had never seen her so interested in the newspaper. She didn't even offer to fix breakfast. This was the greatest compliment of all, Wendy thought. But she was mistaken. Her mother finished the stories just as Wendy was getting ready to leave for school. Wanda got up and hugged Wendy at the door.

"I am so proud of you," she said. "You have done something that will really make a difference."

All day, Wendy felt as if she'd won a prize. The good feelings didn't stop until she got to the *Bugle* that afternoon and found out what Mr. Horton had done. Luella was out on an interview, but Tina greeted her with a grim face.

"Burnam Horton called Luella early this morning," Tina said.

Wendy felt faint and knew the color had probably left her face. "What did he say?"

Tina motioned her to come to her desk, where she punched the "Play" button on a large tape recorder. Wendy recognized Mr. Horton's voice immediately as he started talking.

"Do not run any more stories in that series," the voice growled. As if to shut out the sound, Wendy closed her eyes.

"Who is this?" demanded Luella's voice.

"If you value your own health and that of your workers, and if you want your building not to be damaged in some way, stop publishing that series," said the voice.

Because she had been expecting this call, Luella had the recorder ready and had switched it on when the phone rang. She'd made a copy of the tape for the police.

"What makes Luella think the police will do anything?" Wendy asked Tina.

"What makes you think they won't?"

"They didn't do anything about Roomer, did they?"

"I'm not sure they are through with that investigation, Wendy. Sometimes things take time, especially when you are dealing with a person who has lots of resources. Besides, Luella told them we had proof that Horton was abusing his son."

"What proof?" asked Wendy.

"Your interview. The scars and bruises on his arms. If that's not proof, I don't know what is."

Wendy was scared. She had told Luella everything Burnam said, but she hadn't intended for the police to know. "I didn't mean for her to tell anyone else!" she cried. "What if Burnam's father finds out and does something even worse to Burnam?"

Tina bit her bottom lip. "I'm sure I wasn't supposed to tell you. Luella knew that was a risk, Wendy, but no one can do anything about this kind of abuse unless the victim is willing to tell someone who can do something about it. As long as it's a secret, the abuser is protected. You of all people know that. It's been your argument for running the series."

She put her hands on Wendy's arms and looked into her face. "Don't worry. Let the police do their job."

But Wendy did worry. She thought about all the things that might happen to Burnam until she lost her appetite. For two days, she could eat only small bites of food at dinner, even though she hadn't eaten much all day. Her mother never said a word, even though Wendy's plate looked almost as full after dinner as before. It was as if she was inside Wendy's head.

On Friday before school, Luella called her at home. Her shaking voice scared Wendy. "You need to tell everyone at school not to come in today."

"OK." For the second time in two days, Wendy felt faint. She tried to sound normal. "But everyone will want to know why."

"Just tell them not to come. I will give you all the details later, but I can't talk now."

Fear washed over Wendy, but she willed her voice not to shake. "OK, Luella. I will tell everybody." There was click and Luella was gone.

At school, Mrs. Martino let Wendy make an announcement to the class, minus Burnam, whose desk was empty. Wendy wanted to run out of the school, hop on her bike and ride over to Burnam's house. What was going on?

All day her worry alternated between what had happened to make Luella call, and what had happened to Burnam. She seemed destined to spend her evening the same way. She ate a few bites of rice and salad at dinner. Then she tried to do her math homework. She couldn't concentrate, and everything on the page ran together.

Finally, she shut the book and went to the family room to see what her parents were doing. Her mother was reading a book and her father a magazine.

Just as she was about to ask them what they thought was going on, the phone rang. Wendy jumped. So did Wanda, who picked up the extension beside her chair after the second ring.

"Yes, uh-huh. Oh," she said. Then "Oh" and "Oh," again. Wendy stared at her face and didn't even realize she was holding her breath. Terry Wright stared, too, holding a magazine page taut with his fingers.

After an eternity, Wanda hung up. She studied the floor, her hand still on the phone receiver.

"Mom? Who was on the phone?" Wendy asked when she could stand the suspense no longer.

Wanda looked at her as if just realizing where she was. "Luella. Mr. Horton has been arrested," she said slowly. "The police got a wiretap on his business phone! They recorded him offering money to someone to have something burned. The person said no, so they thought he might do it himself. They followed him to the *Bugle* office tonight and found him spreading gasoline around the back of the building in the warehouse area."

The word "arrested" hit Wendy between the eyes. Thousands of questions swirled around in her head, but she could not figure out what to ask. She stared at her mother. "So is Burnam OK?" she asked finally. "He wasn't at school today."

"I don't know, Wendy. Luella didn't say anything about Burnam. You want to call his house and find out?"

Wendy nodded and went to her room to get the scrap of blue paper with the Hortons' unlisted phone number from the dresser drawer. She had folded it up into a tiny square and kept it in a flat silver box that Miranda had given her right before she died. Just in case she needed it. She went to the kitchen phone and dialed the number. At some point she was aware of her mother coming in and standing behind her.

The phone rang eight times, though it seemed like eighty, and Wendy was about to hang up when a man's voice answered and said a gruff "Hello!" She started to hang up, then remembered Mr. Horton was in jail.

"Ummm…is Burnam there please?"

"Who's calling?" It was almost a growl. Wendy made a split-second decision that she was not going to hang up until she found out if he was OK.

"I'm a friend of his from school. Wendy Wright. He wasn't there today, and I just heard his father got arrested, and I wanted to find out if—"

"Just a minute!" ordered the voice. Then he must have put his hand over the phone, and Wendy could hear him talking to someone else, but she couldn't make out the words. In a moment a woman's voice greeted her.

"Miss Wright? This is Detective Delgado from the Moffatt Corner Police Department. Burnam isn't here, but he and his mother are fine. I think you will see him in school Monday."

"Will you see him before then?" Wendy asked her.

After a short pause, Detective Delgado said, "Yes, I will see him later on tonight."

"Could you give him a message? Could you tell him Wendy said 'hi' and that she missed him today?"

"I'll be glad to, Wendy. I'm sure he will be glad to get the message."

Wendy slept well for the first time in three nights, and when she awoke the next morning, she couldn't even remember dreaming anything.

Twenty-Three

Myra's Wise Words

One sunny Saturday as Wendy read "Cheeky and Claude" at the kitchen table, she suddenly realized it was funny again. She thought back over the last two months. It had started getting funny once more about the same time other happy events had occurred in Moffatt Corner. The gag was the same old thing about Claude's weight, but the story line was changing. Wendy could tell the pair was getting ready to embark on a new assignment.

In the first panel, the two were dressing for the dedication of a new dog hospital. Claude had had to buy a new trenchcoat because he outgrew the old one. But he told Cheeky, "It just wore out."

"Sure, sure. Around the belt area," Cheeky responded in the second panel.

The third panel showed a miffed Claude heading for the door. "If you don't hurry up, we're going to be late for the dedication of the new dog hospital!" he growled.

The fourth panel showed no words, only a picture: Cheeky giving the rotund Pyrenees a gentle nudge through the door, which was almost too small for him.

Wendy pondered the strip, re-reading it. She could almost predict what would happen next. At the dedication, the two would happen upon a new mystery needing their expertise. But she would have to wait to find out what that was. As she reread the strip, she had the same feeling she'd had several times before, that the author of "Cheeky and Claude" either lived in Moffatt Corner or nearby. Its story line was always a subtle mirror of events happening in town. She'd asked both Tina and Luella who the author was and suggested they do a story about him or her, but both of them had brushed off the suggestion. "Nobody cares about that," they said. She knew there was more to the story, but hadn't been able to figure out what the mystery was.

"You look nice," said Wanda, interrupting Wendy's thoughts. "Ready to go?"

"Yes. I'll be early for my appointment, but maybe that means Myra will get to me earlier."

"Don't count on it. I heard she is booked solid because everyone is going to the grand re-opening reception for the hospital and everyone wants a new hairdo."

Wendy had forgotten about that. She wondered if Luella had remembered to assign someone to cover it.

"Don't worry," said Wanda, reading Wendy's face as she started the car. "Luella is going to be there herself. She and Riley are both going to take pictures. And no, you don't need to help. You just go on and take the day off."

Wanda knew all of this because she had started to work at the *Bugle* full time as a copy editor in July, when Luella began hiring staff again. Luella had been so impressed with the work

Wanda had done on the child abuse series that she'd offered her a job three times in a month. Wanda kept saying she didn't have time. Finally, the third time Luella asked, Wanda asked Wendy what she thought.

"It'd be great, Mom. But you have to watch Luella. If you're not careful, she will have you doing a lot more than copy-editing and you will never get away."

So Wanda had become a *Bugle* employee, too, mostly doing editing but sometimes helping Tina with the books, now that everyone was paid again. In the three months since the series ran, advertising and circulation had increased so much that Luella had decided to publish the *Bugle* five days a week beginning in December. And lately she agreed with Wanda that they would need another copy editor at least part time and had started to search for one.

Almost all the Riddle Middle School regulars still worked there, but they could offer only a few hours each week, and Luella was always asking Wendy to find her more reporters or photographers.

Burnam, who had filled many jobs at the newspaper, was gone. Wendy missed him, but she knew it was for the best. For a time after her story about a victim of child abuse was published, everyone at the *Bugle* went from ignoring Burnam to treating him as if he were made of glass. Then he started taking pictures for the paper, and people began to notice how good they were and forgot the rest.

But that lasted only until his father was released on bail and tried to set his own house on fire with Mrs. Horton and Burnam inside. A neighbor saw him and called police, and the fire was put out before it ever got a good start. And Mr. Horton skipped town.

Right after that, Mrs. Horton decided she and Burnam

should leave Moffatt Corner, too. She didn't tell anyone she was leaving or why, but everyone knew anyway. She was afraid he would come back.

But Burnam had managed to get the word to Wendy in a brief conversation the day before they disappeared. "I don't know where we're going, but it will be some place she feels safe," he had said.

"Will you let me know where you are?" Wendy had asked.

"If I can. She's afraid he'll find us, so we will have to be careful."

Then he was gone. She had gotten a couple of post cards from him, but they had come from different places, so she really didn't know where he was. She was surprised at herself for missing him, but she realized that he'd become her friend, just like Riley and Libby. She hoped he was all right.

"The shelter looks busy today," said Wanda. Her voice brought Wendy back, and she stared as they drove by the full parking lot near the small building that had been remodeled for the new animal shelter. Brigette Weaver's fund-raiser had earned enough for a down payment on the empty building, which had been redone to accommodate animals of all sizes. The shady courtyard was landscaped and fenced to provide extra room outdoors, and the shelter had opened in June even though it wasn't quite finished. Today the brown letters of the sign on front were slowly going up, so that you could read the first three: MIR.

Wendy smiled. She knew the rest of the letters because she'd asked Luella to suggest the name, and the suggestion had been quickly adopted since everyone in town thought Luella was wonderful these days. Because the Miranda Wright Animal Shelter had opened, a veterinarian, the same one who had treated Roomer after his rescue, had moved his practice from

Marlett to Moffatt Corner. His clinic was just around the corner from the new shelter, in an office the former vet had vacated when he left town two years ago.

"Here we are," said Wanda, pulling up to Myra's. "How will you get home?"

"I'll walk. I can use the exercise." Wendy had walked or ridden her bicycle everywhere since her cast came off. She believed the exercise was one of the reasons she was able to get into the clothes she was wearing, the red top and gray skirt her mother had bought her in Marlett. The clothes probably would have fit the day her mother had given them to her, but then she wasn't ready to wear them yet.

Myra was working on a customer when Wendy walked in. She glanced at the door, said "I'll be with you in a minute," then looked a second time.

"Wendy? Is that you? Wow," she said. "Red is certainly your color."

Sitting in Myra's chair a few minutes later, she told her she just wanted it shorter and more stylish. "But easy to take care of," she added.

Myra suggested a blunt cut right around the chin line. "It will emphasize your face," she said, staring at Wendy. "You looked so much younger that first time you were in here. It's hard to believe that was just a few months ago. You have really grown up."

Wendy grinned and started to answer, but Myra's finger went to her lips. Then she pointed to two women under hair dryers a few feet away who were having a conversation. The only way they could hear each other was to talk loudly. But that meant everyone else could hear them, too.Wendy caught the tail end of what Myra must have heard: "...it's all happened since those kids took over at the *Bugle*," said one.

"I hear that chunky little Wright girl, Wanda's kid, is the one who saved that newspaper. Practically single-handedly," her friend replied.

"If you ask me, she saved a lot more than the *Bugle*."

Her companion nodded knowingly, and they returned to their magazines.

"Know what I hear?" said Myra loudly to the women, playfully poking Wendy in the ribs with her styling comb. "I hear she isn't chunky now, either."

"Really?" said the two women in unison, looking up at Myra. "Maybe the *Bugle* will publish her diet plan," suggested one. "I wouldn't mind losing a few pounds." She looked at Wendy. "Red looks good on you, Honey. You should wear it all the time."

"Thank you," said Wendy.

The other one glanced at Wendy and nodded in agreement, then told her friend, "I heard that Wright girl really wasn't all that fat to begin with. That was probably just gossip. Anyway, you want to lose weight? Drinking water is what you want to do." That began a whole new discussion.

"What did I save besides the *Bugle*?" Wendy whispered to Myra.

"The town, probably. That's what I've heard a lot of people say. There's a whole new attitude now that Horton is gone. But you want me to ask them?"

Wendy blushed and shook her head, content for now that someone was saying good things about her, even if they were an exaggeration. She was pleased the *Bugle* was doing well and thought Miranda would be, too. It looked like the *Bugle* would continue publishing for awhile and Wendy planned to work there until she left Moffatt Corner for college.

She was bored, though, with how smoothly things were

going now. It was better than before, but there wasn't enough to do with no problems to solve.

She was as relieved as everyone else that Mr. Horton was gone. He had been like a poison weed, choking out all the good growth. But Wendy knew that sometimes aggressive weeds grew back. She tried to put the thought out of her head, but she must have sighed because Myra wanted to know if something was the matter.

"Not really, I guess."

"Just remember that nothing's ever perfect. Be glad if you just get close." Myra winked at her.

Wendy thought of Burnam when Myra said that. "I am glad," she said, "and I know someone else who is, too."

Myra smiled and nodded as if she knew exactly the person.

"Hey, Myra," said Wendy suddenly as a thought occurred to her. "Do you read 'Cheeky and Claude' in the *Bugle*?"

"Every time the paper comes out. I got so upset when I thought they were going to take it out! Now don't get mad, but I think that's one of the paper's best features!"

"You're right. But who do you think the author is?"

"Don't you know?" Myra asked with a funny look on her face.

Wendy started to say no, but something about Myra's look made her hold back. "I just wanted to know if you knew," she hedged.

"Myra doesn't know!" yelled one of the women from her dryer. "We've been discussing that in here since that strip started! You try to read the name on it. It's just a scribble! You can't make it out! No one in town knows who the author is!"

Myra winked at Wendy again. "Something new for you to investigate," she said. "Now, is this about the right length?" she asked as she turned Wendy's head slightly to the side.

Wendy nodded, even though she barely heard. She was going to the *Bugle* after all today, to start on a new story. She was sure Luella wouldn't mind after Wendy showed her how it would bring in readers.

THE END